TRANSCONTINENTAL BREAKFAST

THUNDERTAIL SLAPBUSH

Cover design: Ami Agisi

Managing editor: Diane Callahan, QuotidianWriter.com

Copy editor: Angela Traficante, LambdaEditing.com

 Created with Vellum

Content note:

If I don't know what meal you are, how will I know when to eat you?

Very little about this book is serious, dear reader, but there is one thing that I want to make very clear: Homestyle's identity as a transgender individual is *not* the punchline. The absurdity of gender gatekeeping absolutely is.

So, let's get this out of the way. If you're in favor of the laws being bandied about right now, or have anything negative to say about the trans and nonbinary communities as a whole? This book is not for you. I didn't write it with you in mind, and you're not going to like it. Toodle-oo. Off you pop. Have a lovely day and thanks for saving us both a headache later.

Still here? Excellent. I hope you have a strange sense of humor and/or a strong stomach. I'm not okay and I doubt you are either, but we'll get through this together.

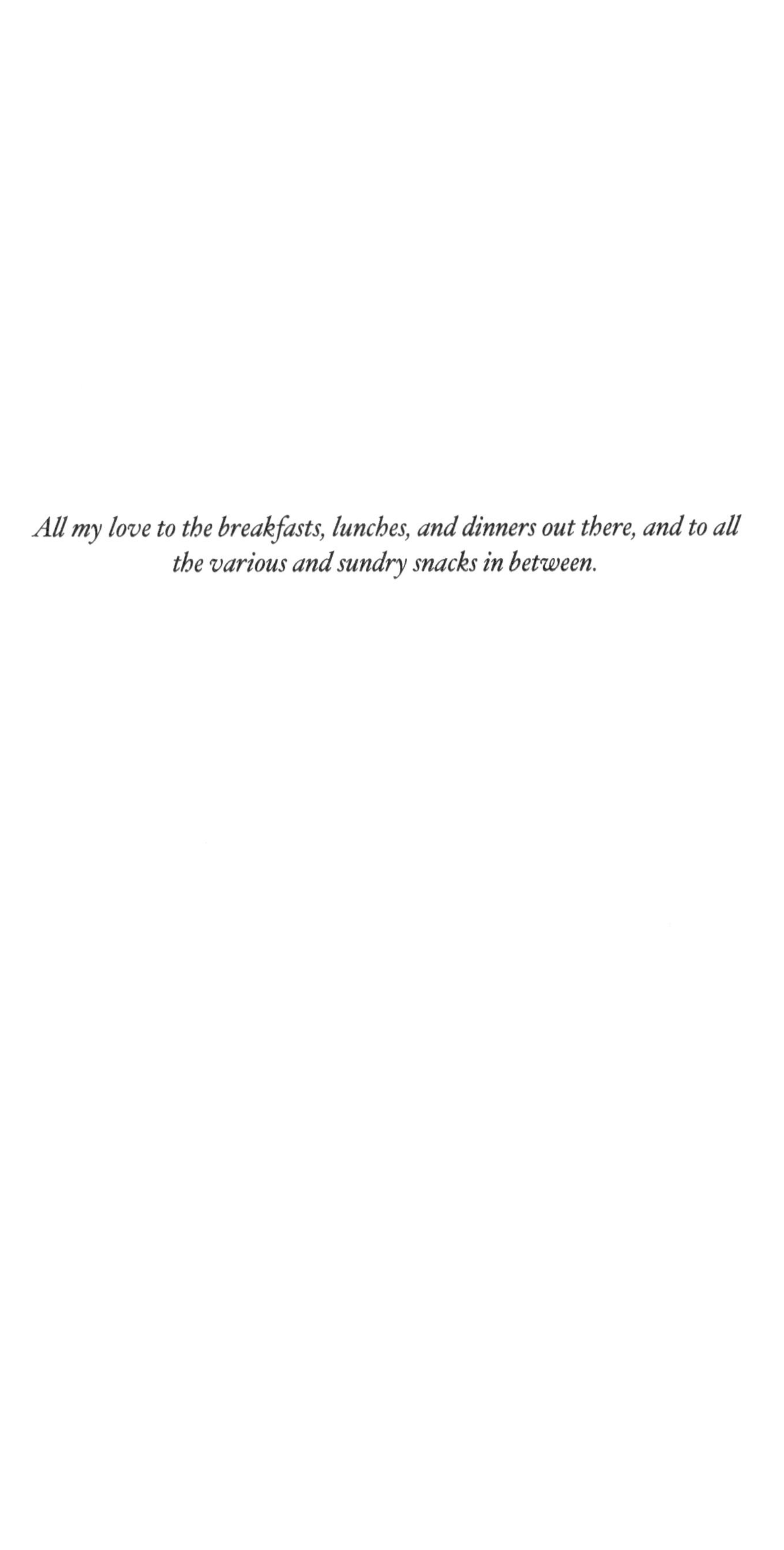

All my love to the breakfasts, lunches, and dinners out there, and to all the various and sundry snacks in between.

Chapter One

It's the brats of times, it's the wurst of times, and I'm running myself ragged at the back of the Pig-in-a-Poke breakfast bistro. The bacon is crisping on the griddle, and so am I. The air in the kitchen is so hot I feel like I'm boiling alive.

Philosophers have long speculated about what happened to make us the way we are. The question of cannibalism is tossed around a lot in college courses and debate clubs. The phrase *you are what you eat* is often offered as an explanation, although that's clearly not the case. Exhibit A: I didn't have time to eat before I left the house today, and yet here I am, a bowl of chicken-and-mustard-green rice congee. Which, for the record, is also the special today.

The way I see it, you are what you *feel*. This morning, for example, I was feeling a little nostalgic, unexpectedly complex, more savory than sweet, and somewhat out of place in the city. I blame my mood last night. I sat on the balcony of my little apartment long into the evening, listening to recordings of some of my mom's favorite songs from when she was a little girl growing up in Thailand. My relationship with my mother is complicated, just like my recipe this morning. It took a long time to get ready, and I was almost late for work, which isn't a good look when you run your own restaurant.

"How are you holding up, Nat?" India sticks her head through the kitchen door to check in on me. She's a fairly new hire, but she picked up the routine of the Pig-in-a-Poke in a matter of weeks. Today, she's a perky finger millet idli. I should ask her for her recipe sometime.

"Almost there, right?" I check the clock. We're only open for another hour. My heart sinks as I realize that, once again, nobody's ordered the special. I keep trying to mix up the menu, but no matter how hard I try, nobody bites. I'm determined not to let it get me down. People find comfort in the familiar.

India checks her notepad, types the new order into the POS, and flashes me a grin. "You're going to love this one."

The printer buzzes, and I try not to groan when I see that we have yet another double order for the quiche Lorraine. "Doesn't *anyone* want to try anything new?"

"People order the *huevos rancheros* all the time," India says kindly.

"That doesn't count," I grumble. At least India understands where I'm coming from. International cuisines don't get the same love as the more "American" dishes, and I say that with the most exaggerated air quotes possible. Once upon a time, quiche Lorraine and huevos rancheros were international dishes, but they've been embraced by the general public, while foods like congee and idli are still considered "exotic."

"They like what's familiar," India says.

That's what I've been wrestling with ever since I opened Pig-in-a-Poke. How do we get people to branch out and acquaint themselves with the *un*familiar when they're so stuck in their ways?

The question bothers me right up until closing time, when the last of our diners shuffle out and we can finally lock up.

"Well, well, well, International Fusion, what do you think?" My front-of-house manager beams at me. Aside from my parents, he's the only one who gets to use my full name. That's the privilege of being my first hire, compounded by the fact that he's old enough to be my dad. "Another successful breakfast rush. How much longer until you're ready to establish a franchise?"

Full English, known to his friends as Monty, doesn't always get the struggle like India does. He's steady, though, a reliably filling heart attack on a plate. I can be more honest with him than I am even with some of my friends.

"I don't know." I slump against the counter, so exhausted that I almost slop a bit of rice porridge over the edge of my bowl. I pull the dish towel out of my apron pocket and dab at my forehead as I continue. "I love this place, Monty, but it's not what I thought it would be. I wanted it to be *special*. Why bother franchising if it's just going to be another run of the mill break-fast spot?"

Monty eyes me shrewdly. "You could always try the pop-up idea."

Ah, the pop-up. My other brainchild, the one that I've been kicking around for the last two years. Truth be told, I don't need to be on-site to make the Pig-in-a-Poke run smoothly. Anyone could be back there on the griddle. I don't even work weekends anymore, not since I was able to hire a guy to pick up the slack. A couple years back, it occurred to me that I could run a pop-up event once or twice a month and serve a curated menu of hand-picked international dishes, designed not only to showcase unfa-miliar flavors, but to show how *well* things can go together. As the daughter of a Thai immigrant and a second-generation Brazilian entrepreneur, fusion has always been my *thing*. A little bit of this, a little bit of that, and all of it with a distinctly Amer-ican twist.

I believe in my cooking. What I doubt is the willingness of the general public to try something new. I don't want to be seen as an outsider, or lock myself into a niche. But at this rate, I'm locking myself into a life of bland uniformity, so am I really coming out ahead?

Monty snaps his fingers. "My dear, you've gone positively

vacant. My apologies. I didn't mean to pressure you. I'm just worried that you're holding yourself back. We both know that you can do better than tired French knockoffs and sunny-side-ups. Just think about it."

"It's such a big commitment," I groan.

"You have the capital. If you tried it for six months and it failed, well then, at least you gave it the old what for." Monty winks at me.

"Yes," I retort, well aware of how much I sound like a petulant child, "but then I'd know that it wouldn't work."

Monty sniffs. "You mean that instead of merely *doubting* yourself, you'd have confirmation of your disappointment?"

I dab my face again. "Exactly."

In the dining room, India is just finishing up her sidework. "Not that I'm eavesdropping or whatever," she calls, "but for what it's worth, I still think the pop-up would be rad as hell."

I close my eyes and let the fantasy play out again. A multi-course chef's tasting menu of fry jacks and *nasi lemak* with sambal, beef, and roasted peanuts, or quick-pickled vegetables alongside a savory meat-stuffed *burek*...

There would be no point in putting those words on a menu, since 90 percent of my usual customers won't know what they mean, but if I could just get their butts in the seats long enough to give them a taste, I'm sure they'd be hooked.

Maybe it's worth a shot.

A quick *tap-tap-tap* on the glass of the front door, like the eager pecking of a pigeon, makes Monty groan. "Your friend is here."

I don't have to ask who he means. Outside of work, I don't have a lot of friends, and Keto and I have a standing date on Tuesdays.

Sure enough, the owner of the juice bar across the street is standing just outside, waving furiously. Today, she's half an avocado stuffed with a soft-boiled egg, topped with cheese, and sprinkled with bacon bits.

"Be nice," I tell Monty as I head to the door and unlock it.

"Ohmygosh*hiyouguys!*" Keto bounds into the room. "Did you have an amazing day? Are we manifesting good things?"

India leans on her broom and does her best not to roll her eyes. "Hey, Keto."

"Oh my goodness!" Keto claps her hands in excitement. "So cute today, India, you're always *soooo* exotic, I love it. And girl, get a load of this!" She snaps her fingers in my general direction. "Killer look! A little high on carbs, so not for me, but you know I love you anyway." She plants air kisses on my cheeks. Behind her back, Monty pretends to heave.

I get why he and India don't like Keto. She can be... a lot. It would be nice if she would check her privilege a little more often, and I could go the rest of my life without her ever calling any of us "exotic" again or making a comment about my health benefits. That aside, she was the first local restaurateur to accept me after I moved here to start Pig-in-a-Poke, and she's helped me navigate the ups and downs of being a young female business owner in a new city. She's not perfect, but she tries.

I hug her gingerly, careful not to spill any of my taboo carbs on her. "Hey, Keto. New recipe?"

"What, this old thing?" Keto strikes a pose. "No, girl, this is a classic. It's practically *vintage.* Not like whatever *you've* got going on, how *novel.*"

I bite my tongue and spare her the lecture on the topic of the centuries-old dish that ultimately developed into congee, or how many people consume it on a regular basis across vast swathes of the world. Keto's worldview can be remarkably narrow, but she means well.

That's what I tell myself, anyway.

Across the room, India blinks vapidly at me. "Yeah, Nat, how inventive of you."

"Thanks," I say belatedly. "Sorry Keto, can you give me, like, two minutes? I just want to do a last walk-through of the kitchen and grab my stuff from the back."

"Girl, *please.*" Keto flaps one hand at me and perches on the edge of the counter alongside the register. "Take your time."

Monty gives me one last searching look as I dip through the kitchen door. I get where he's coming from, I really do. But the fact remains that business and fantasy don't always overlap. My coworkers might support me, but there are a lot of people in the city who think the way Keto does, and they don't even try to be nice about it.

I want to be successful. I want to do my parents proud. I dread the idea of putting my whole heart into something only to watch it fail.

But I'm starting to wonder if that line of thinking means that my whole heart will end up going to waste like the ingredients I set aside for the congee special that nobody ordered today.

Chapter Two

"Wow." The businessman across the counter looks me up and down. The egg-wrap of his breakfast burrito body is as tightly wound as his attitude, and it's all stuffed into a dark navy suit that probably cost him more than I make in a month. "Are they so desperate for help that they'll hire anyone these days?"

Some days, dealing with costumers like him makes me angry, but today it just makes me tired. *I don't need your commentary on my appearance, thank you very much. We don't need to whip our sausages out and measure. Just tell me what kind of coffee you want and piss off.*

I can't say that, though. I need this job, so shitty customer or not, I force a weary smile onto my face. "What size coffee would you like, sir?"

The man narrows his eyes and then, with a glint of evil glee, says, "Medium, double shot of espresso, two pumps hazelnut and one of gingerbread, oat milk, foam cap, and three taps of cocoa powder to finish. You got all that?" He speaks so fast that his words all run together.

"Yes, sir," I say wearily.

He leers. "You gonna write that down, son?"

I stare at him for a solid three seconds before lurching into action. Guys like this take one look at me and assume that all I'm good for is taking notes and making change. I know it's not the *healthiest* possible attitude, but I'm already determined to prove this guy wrong by making him the best damn medium-double-shot-two-pumps-nuts-one-ginger oat milk latte that has ever passed his smug, condescending lips—foam cap and all.

I thought my life would be better after I came out, and in some ways, it has been. Even egg-faces like this ding-dong get my pronouns right these days. Not that he deserves a gold star for what should be common courtesy, but it's something.

What really gets me is that no matter what I do, no matter how many orders I get right, no matter how many pristine coffees topped with adorable foam art that I pour, people still see me and think, *Oh, he's a dinner.*

I'm not a dinner, goddamnit, no matter what people assume. I never have been. I spent most of my life living a lie, and now that I'm finally living my truth, people still think it's up for debate.

Egg-wrap guy watches in silence as I spin through the shop, making him the perfect drink. At last, I plonk his cup in front of him and hold out my hand for his card.

He glances from the drink to my face. "You didn't ask if I wanted it to go."

Because I didn't want you to stay in this shop a moment longer than necessary, I think, but I just smile sweetly. "I can see that you're a busy guy with places to be. I read between the lines."

He nods his approval before handing over his card, then he signs the screen. He even tips. I'd like to think that he's riddled with guilt for being a walking douchecanoe, but in all probability, he's just decided that I'm *one of the good ones* and moved on with his day. I wish people's microaggressions didn't bother me as much as they do, but here we are.

He takes a sip of his latte and nods. "Thanks," he says, before turning on his Italian leather heel and strutting out the front door.

I hate people like that.

Still, there's not much I can do. Instead, I focus on cleaning up the little baking area behind and to the right of the register. All of our workspaces are right out in the open, which means that I don't have to abandon the register to tidy up. Most of our sales come from coffee, but I've had to brush up on my baking skills since I started working at The Daily Grind. My boss is an absolute caffeine fiend. A few months ago, one of her friends dared her to get the words *Death Before Decaf* tattooed across her forehead, and three days later, she jittered through the door with her new tat peeking from below her bangs. I'll never reach her level of fanaticism, but at least I can pour a coffee on her level now.

Our little oven is mostly clean when the bell on the door front door chimes. I turn to make sure that it's not one of our customers leaving and almost drop my sponge.

It's *her*.

I was in such a rush this morning, I completely forgot that it was Tuesday. I can't believe that I left the house as hash browns on a *Tuesday*. It's a perfectly respectable breakfast food, nothing fancy, but that's the problem. She always looks amazing. I don't recognize her appearance today, but it's some sort of translucent porridge studded with bits of braised chicken and bright green scallions. I close my eyes and take a whiff of her, hoping that she won't notice, and my stomach rumbles at the perfume of tangy rice vinegar, umami aged soy sauce, and bright anise that heralds her arrival at the counter. My mouth waters, and for one moment, I fantasize about dipping myself into her wet warmth and swallowing a whole mouthful of her chunky sweetness.

Down, boy. I have to literally press my palm to my watering mouth as she approaches. Every time she walks through the door, I'm overcome with this hungry—almost ravenous—feeling. I don't like it. If she felt the same way, it would be fine, but get real. A girl like her would never go for a guy like me.

Not that it stops me from wanting to take a bite out of her.

Fortunately, she's so engrossed in her conversation with her friend that she doesn't notice the way I'm watching her.

The avocado is saying, "I'm trying this new diet now, ya know? It's, like, *totally* slimming. No grains, no nuts, no oils, only all-natural whole foods."

"Mm-hmm." My dreamgirl nods, but I can see that she's entertained by this diatribe. I've never quite been able to work out their vibe, but they're cute together.

Of course, my dreamgirl is plenty cute on her own. Too bad they never order their drinks to go. It means I get to look at her longer, but I never have the chance to ask her name.

The avocado turns to me and glances up at the menu, as if they haven't been coming to The Daily Grind for at least as long as I've worked here. "I'll have a raspberry mochaccino, no whipped cream, *no milk*." She makes sure to catch my eye. "This is important, I'm on a super strict diet, all right?"

"Got it." I nod seriously, trying not to smile when my dream-girl catches my eye and grins. Right, because raspberry syrup and mocha blends are a health food. "And for you?"

"I'll take a shot in the dark with a little cream." Dreamgirl beams at me.

My hash-brown heart patters against my ribs. God, she could make *anything* sound sexy. "Yeah," I squeak. Then an idea occurs to me, one so obvious that I wonder why I haven't done it before. "If you want to give me your names and pay now, I can bring your drinks over to you when they're done. The, uh, mochaccinos sometimes take a while."

"Oh, totally." The avocado bobs her head. "I'm Keto."

Dreamgirl eyes me up. "And I'm Nat."

Nat. Nat. Nat. Her name bobs around in my head. It's so short and so perfect for her.

Keto pays first, still regaling Nat with the details of her new wonder-diet. When it's Nat's turn to pay, her palm brushes mine as she takes her change.

"Thank you..." Her eyes flick to my name tag. "Homes."

"Huh." I make a sound like I'm giggling, but it warbles in my throat. "Huh huh huh. I'll, um, have your drinks ready in a moment."

They head to their usual table by the window, although I catch Nat glancing back at me as they walk. I can't tell if we're in on the joke about her friend's diet, or if I *am* the joke, but I can't say that I care. Right now, I'd do anything for her.

I wish I understood what it is about her that draws me in like a fly to honey. My hands shake as I make their drinks, and I keep glancing at her over the top of the espresso machine.

I try to make Keto's drink as nice as possible so that it won't seem strange when I pour a microfoam heart onto the surface of Nat's cup. I deliver them myself, carefully placing each beverage in the center of the table so that I won't spill a drop.

"Thank you, Homes," Nat says, meeting my eyes this time.

"Y-you're welcome," I stammer, before scurrying back behind the counter. Did we have a moment? I think we had a moment.

She barely glances at me again through the rest of the conversation, but when they bring their cups back up to the counter just before closing, she catches my eye and grins.

I'm lost. I'm shipwrecked on the Isle of Nat, totally in love with a food group who's way out of my league.

Still, I remember how my name sounded on her lips, and I can't stop smiling.

Leftovers is lying on the couch when I get home, smoking a joint as he watches reruns of *Entrée-You*.

"Hey," he rasps when I open the door. "Was she there today? It's Tuesday, right?"

"She *was*." I drop onto the couch beside him. Most people think Leftovers is kind of a bum, and I'm not saying they're wrong, but he's a genuinely good guy. When I first came out as breakfast, everyone told me that I was going through a phase. *You're just breakfast for dinner sometimes. It's natural to experiment.* Leftovers was the only one who got me. He's gone through phases of being breakfast, lunch, *and* dinner, so he's basically the guru of subverting the mealtime trinary. Lately, he's been breakfast most of the time, but I support him no matter *what* meal he is. We're tight like that.

"Did you grow a pair of Scotch eggs and actually *talk* to her this time?" he asks, his eyes never leaving the screen. He's got the volume set way, way down low, so that I can't hear what Guy Hungry is saying, but I've seen enough of the show to get the gist. His whole schtick is shaming people for their recipes, even though he's a TV dinner. Reality TV is friggin' weird. I don't see the appeal.

"I asked for her name," I say.

That gets his attention. He looks over at me with bloodshot pepperoni eyes. "*Noice,* dude." He holds out one fist, and we bump knuckles. "And?"

"Nat," I sigh.

"Nat," Leftovers repeats. "Right on. How about her number?"

"Uh." I pick at the crispy edges of my fried potato straws. "Nooo, not yet, not exactly."

Leftovers groans extravagantly and flops back against the arm of the couch. "No, my dude! I'm telling you, you gotta shoot your shot!"

I squirm against the cushions. "What if she thinks I'm weird?"

"You frickin' *are* weird, Homestyle. That's cool. I know you're weird, and I still like you."

"Yeah," I point out, "but you don't want to eat me."

Leftovers snorts and takes another drag of his joint. "You sure about that, my guy? I'll go right now. Just say the word."

"Oh, shut up." I smack him. "You know what I mean."

"Yeah, I do." He lets out a puff of smoke that curls in wisps toward the ceiling. "I just worry about you. I'm telling you, go out to a club, meet some nice dish who'll stroke your sausage a couple times or get their custard all over your spotted dick or whatever you're into, and once you know your way around the kitchen, *then* go after the real meal."

We've had this argument before. I get the logic of what he's saying, but even if I didn't have a romantic fantasy or two of my own, I can't imagine pairing up with some random side dish. I don't want *someone*—I want *her*.

When he sees my expression, Leftovers sighs. "Hey, forget it. You don't need to do anything different, you know? But you *do* need to make a move, because she has no idea who you are. The least she can do is turn you down, and you won't be any worse than you are now." He turns back to the TV, where Guy Hungry has reduced some poor lunch entrée to tears.

He has a point, but as I get up from the couch, all my happiness from the encounter drains away. My friend is right. I have no experience to speak of. I wouldn't even know what to do if she agreed to a date, much less if she wanted to do anything more intimate. I drag myself to my room and flop down on the bed, staring up at the popcorn ceiling while the TV drones in the next room.

"Hello," I whisper. "I'm Homes. I mean, you know that. No, wait, let's try again. Hi, I'm short for Homestyle—oh my God, no, that doesn't even make sense. Hey, girl, I want to lick you all over... *Shit.*"

I squeeze my eyes shut. How do people do this? How do they flirt? How do they ask each other out and not sound like absolute animals?

It's the truth, though, right? I think. *You do want to lick her. You want to taste her on your tongue, spread yourself between her thighs like clotted cream on a minimuffin. You want to drizzle her biscuits with your gravy, you want to layer your vanilla parfait between scoops of her fruit salad...*

And of course, my body responds.

"No," I groan, rolling onto my belly. Lord knows why I think this would help, because my sausage casing is already sensitive to even the slightest touch. I am *not* going to entertain lewd fantasies about her. That would be crass.

Not as crass as smothering her eggs with your hollandaise would be, my filthy mind supplies.

My sausage is sizzling, and I give into temptation. Before

long, a savory aroma fills the room, ripe with fennel and sage, undercut with the primal tang of smoked pork. Leftovers is going to be able to smell exactly what I'm up to in here, but I can't help myself, not when I think of *her*. I wriggle out of my cargo shorts and rub my ithyphallic pork against the sheets, leaving a greasy stain with each stroke. I imagine dousing her cheerios with my whole milk and drenching her French toast in my heavy cream.

I may not have had the guts to shoot my shot at the café, but it isn't long before I shoot something else as I dig my fingers deeper into the sheets, bite back my guilty cries of pleasure, and whisper her name as I finish.

Chapter Three

Tuesday rolls around again, and not only have I completely failed to make peace with my life choices, I'm in a crumby mood over the fact that some lady sent her breakfast back because apparently she expected India to set her butter pats on the toaster while I was cooking. They were, and I quote, *not sufficiently pre-softened.*

"It's fucking scrambled eggs and toast," I grumble. "Are you seriously telling me that she couldn't make this herself if the *butter consistency* was that big a deal?"

Monty winks at me. "Don't complain, Nat. People like her are your bread and butter." He winks extravagantly and shoots me finger guns.

I point to him, then hook my finger to wave him closer. "Come say that again when your beans are within slapping range."

He giggles to himself as he dashes back out of the kitchen.

I spend the rest of the morning oscillating between the conviction that people like this would *never* warm up to my tasting menu idea, and the conflicting but equally strong belief that I am sacrificing my soul by even contemplating the palates of the absolute Karens infesting my beloved restaurant. By the time we finally close, I'm considering giving up on the restaurant industry altogether. Maybe I could become a food blogger and travel the world.

"Are you and Keto going out today?" India asks. Today, she's a green chili uttapam.

"As far as I know."

India waves the broom handle in my direction. "I hope you're prepared for a lecture about the pitfalls of both gluten *and* cheese."

She's not wrong. Before my day went to shit, I was light and airy as *pão de queijo*, so I am indeed a cheesy breadball. "At least I'm not too exotic," I mutter. My words are followed by a stab of guilt. Keto isn't perfect, but if I want her to alter her behavior, I should say something to her face rather than gossip about her behind her back.

As if summoned by my thoughts, Keto raps on the front door. She's some kind of bacon frittata today, which is pretty standard fare. I'm surprised to see that she's not alone. Standing beside her is a gloriously messy concoction of waffle, ice cream, and chocolate sauce.

"Ooh." India's face heats up. "Brunch is here? I didn't know *she* was coming today."

"Don't even think about it," I warn India. "I love her dearly, but she's a mess. You do *not* want to get involved."

"Mhmm." India sighs dreamily as Brunch's ice cream drips onto the pavement. "I hear what you're saying, but look at her."

"Say it with me: *guaranteed regret*." I take India by the shoulders and force her to look me in the eyes. "Do not. Fuck. The waffle."

"But she's scrumptious," India whines.

I spin toward Monty. "Talk some sense into this girl, please."

Monty, who is doing a crossword puzzle in pen at the register, doesn't even glance up. "You only live once, darling."

I roll my eyes as I walk past him to get the door. "Not helpful."

"*NAT!*" Keto bounds into the room. I wish I had her energy.

"Oh my gosh, girl, you look good as always. Does that recipe make you look a little *round?* Sure! But guys love a curvy girl."

I'm suddenly glad that Brunch is here. I could go for something stronger than a coffee, and Brunch loves to party. I can count on one hand the number of times we've met up where she hasn't at least *tried* to sell us on the idea of mimosas and Bloody Marys.

Brunch drifts over toward India, who's still staring. "Hey there," she purrs. "How are you doing?"

"Um," India says. I swear, the child is drooling.

"No harassing the employees," I call. "I *am* the HR department, remember?"

"If you don't want me to flirt, then you shouldn't have hired such a cute little dish." Brunch winks at India.

"Okay, we're leaving!" I loop my arm through Keto's, thankful that I grabbed my purse earlier. I would hate to abandon India to her fate. Everything about Brunch screams trouble, but for some people, that's a siren song.

"Later, cutie." Brunch winks and saunters toward the door, leaving India staring after her open mouthed.

When we're out on the street, I click my tongue at Brunch. "Go easy on the poor girl, huh? She's a good kid. Don't lead her on."

Brunch holds up both hands in self-defense. "Hey, now. I've never been anything but perfectly honest about my intentions. I'm not looking for commitment. I'm a wine-'em-and-dine-'em kinda gal. She's a big girl. She can decide for herself if she wants one wild, sloppy ride on the ol' tea trolley."

"Wow." I shudder. "I will literally *pay you money* never to say those words again."

Keto snickers. "Tea trolley," she repeats. "Nice."

People on the street are staring at us, and I'm not sure if it's because they're eavesdropping on us, or if they're simply drawn to Brunch. Trainwreck she may be, but there's something about her that draws people to her. Like it or not, I'm pulled into her orbit just as much as anyone else. She's so authentically *herself,* and she's right: she's never pretended to be anything but what she is. Instead of trying to make herself look respectable in the eyes of the general public, she's embraced her identity. She *flaunts* it.

I'd never admit it, but I'm extraordinarily jealous. There's nothing braver than being true to yourself, and Brunch walks the walk. If I had her bravery, my pop-up would already be up and running, and if anyone gave me lip about it, I'd kick them to the curb and keep walking.

"How have you been?" I ask Brunch.

"Oh, you know." She drags one finger through her melting *à la mode* and licks the sweet cream absently. "Late nights, late mornings, nonstop parties. I'm telling you, life as an influencer is a dream. I'm getting sponsorship offers left and right."

"That's so cool!" Keto gushes.

"I'm really happy for you," I say, and I mean it. When I first met Brunch, she had just dropped out of college and was struggling to get by. The fact that she's managed to find her niche gives me hope that I'll find mine one day.

As we approach our usual spot, Keto wriggles out of my grip to hold the door open for us. "You're gonna love this place, Brunch. We come here all the time."

Brunch squints up at the oversized menu that hangs on the back wall. "Do they have mimosas?"

Keto and I exchange a grin. It's always odd to be partly on the outside, partly on the inside. I'm not sure that Keto even realizes how condescending she can be sometimes.

You could tell her, I think, but to be honest, I don't see that happening. What if she decided that I was the problem and dropped me like a hot 'tot? I would be pretty much alone in the city. I don't know how I would cope.

I need to get my head right. "Why don't you two order?" I suggest. "I'm going to run to the bathroom."

"We'll be at our usual table!" Keto chirps.

Brunch is already asking the barista questions. As I shuffle off to the unisex bathroom in the back corner of the restaurant,

I happen to glance up and make eye contact with Homes. He's here most weeks.

To be honest, I didn't pay that much attention at first. There was nothing particularly eye-catching about him, and we only spoke long enough for me to order and pay. After a few visits, though, I caught him watching me from behind the register a few times. Whenever I made eye contact, he turned away and got all flustered. It was kind of...

Cute, I guess. So I started noticing more.

I flash him a quick smile before hurrying back to the restroom. I lock the door behind me and lean against the sink, staring at myself in the mirror. I should have known that Keto would have an opinion about my recipe today. But who cares? I bet she had a few choice words for Brunch, too. Carbs, dairy, sugar, presentation... no doubt Brunch got an earful, although I doubt she let it get under her waffle.

Did she, though? Some of my old doubts about my friends creep in. Keto loves attention, and when she's with Brunch, people notice her. Would she risk driving a wedge between herself and her "famous" friend?

Or does she save all of her veiled insults for me, because she knows I'll put up with it?

I hate being so insecure. I hate caring so much what people think.

I hate how desperate I am for approval.

"Get your shit together," I tell my reflection. The *pão de queijo* in the mirror glares back at me, looking just the right amount of salty. "Stop being a bitch. It's not Keto's fault that you're insecure, and it's not her job to fix you. Figure yourself out."

Despite having done nothing but stand in front of the mirror, I flush the toilet and wash my hands, just in case anyone's standing outside, even while hating that I bother to put on this little performance of normalcy for no one. Surely this level of self-consciousness is unusual?

I open the door and hurry out to the counter. Brunch and

Keto are already sitting at our table by the window, chatting animatedly about something or other. I *want* to be excited about being out with them, but the idea of putting on a show of happiness leaves me exhausted even before I join in the conversation.

Homes is waiting at the counter, already smiling at me. There's something about him that seems awfully *young*, but maybe it's just his relentless positivity. He's always smiling. Today, he's a plain bagel with what looks like pimento spread.

"Hey, Nat," he says. His cheeks are slightly more toasted than before. "The usual, right?" He pushes a mug toward me.

I freeze. Instead of his usual foam art, he's painstakingly written out a number in cream.

"Oh," I breathe. "Um... yeah."

"On the house," he says, and quickly turns away, snatching up a rag so that he can wipe down what, to me, looks like a pristine stretch of counter.

"Thanks," I say, hoping that he'll turn around to acknowledge me. He doesn't.

I pick up my mug and walk back to the table, keeping my steps steady so that I won't disturb the surface of the drink. I'm not sure what to make of this.

When I slide into the empty chair, Keto and Brunch turn to greet me. Keto's eyes widen as she points one perfectly manicured fingernail at my drink.

"*What*," she asks frostily, "is *that?*"

"I think the barista gave me his number," I mumble.

"Ooh." Brunch leans back to peer at Homes. She's not even subtle about it. "Okay. I'm not seeing a lot of *flavor* there, but I appreciate boldness. Is he...?"

"Yeah," Keto says.

The two of them share a knowing look and sip their drinks in unison.

"What?" I ask, leaning over the table and lowering my voice. "You know something about him? Spill the tea."

"I'm pretty sure he wasn't always, you know." Brunch bounces her eyebrows.

"What? A guy?" I spin in my chair to look at Homes again. That makes sense, actually. It explains some of the vibes I've gotten from him, but that doesn't make him any less of a hunk.

"Yeah, but that's whatever." Keto waves a dismissive hand. "The real tea? He wasn't always *breakfast*."

I turn back to her and frown. "Meaning?"

"Meaning that he was born a... *dinner.*" Keto doesn't say the last word, she just mouths it exaggeratedly.

"Oh." I frown down at my untouched coffee. "Okay."

"Not that there's anything wrong with being dinner," Keto adds hurriedly. "But it's weird, right? I mean, stay in your meal. It's, like, total breakfast appropriation."

"Wow." Brunch's eyebrows shoot up. "I didn't know you were such a TERB."

"I'm *not* a TERB," Keto snaps. "I just like natural breakfasts."

"Again—wow." Brunch puffs out her cheeks and looks down into her half-empty mug. "Big yikes."

"Well, I'm sorry I'm not woke like you," Keto retorts.

I'm not really familiar with the terms they're throwing around. I've *heard* them, of course, but they don't mean much to me. People on the news talk about meal-transition all the time, but I've never met a transcontinental breakfast in real life. Not that I know of, anyway.

While Keto and Brunch bicker, I slide my phone out of my bag. The foam has cooled down and dissipated into my coffee, but the numbers are still legible. I snap a photo while my friends aren't looking.

Keto has an opinion about what it means for Homes to be who he is. But she also has opinions about me and India. I'm not sure that I plan to text him, but at the very least, I'm going to form my own opinion.

I know what it's like to be different, and I'm not convinced that it's a bad thing.

· · ·

By the time I stumble in the door, my head is spinning. Instead of being exhausted, I'm full of questions. I kick off my shoes and flop down on the couch with my laptop. Time to see what Goo can teach me.

The trouble is, I'm not sure *what* to Goo. After some consideration, I type in, *Cute guy used to be dinner.* Most of what populates are personal anecdotes from EatIt, a Wikimealdia page, and some videos from DoxxNews. I skip over Doxx and work my way through the other pages. It doesn't take me long to work out that a TERB is a Transcontinental-Exclusionary Radical Breakfast.

An hour later, I set my laptop aside, feeling not much the wiser. I don't understand what people get so bent out of shape about. Honestly, it seems pretty straightforward: Homes was raised as a dinner girl, and in reality, he's a breakfast guy. Why should anyone think that they know him better than he knows himself? It sounds like the same sort of gatekeeping crap that Keto pulls with me sometimes. In short, none of the TERB logic makes any sense to me—sounds like a bunch of insecure bullshit, in fact—and it doesn't impact my interest in Homes.

Which begs the question: *am* I interested in Homes?

I stare up at the ceiling and let my eyes unfocus, trying to picture him clearly. He's always been kind of quiet. He fades into the background. Now, I wonder if he does that to keep people like Keto from taking too much notice of him. I imagine his pale bagel crust from this morning, how I could run my lips and teeth over him, taking a little nibble of him here and there. I could slip my tongue between his halves and lick out mouthfuls of his thick, creamy pimento spread...

I've been on my own too long, because the idea of his pimento cheese smeared over my lips and chin instantly toasts me. I let my fingers trail over my perfectly cooked exterior until I find that sweet spot, then press my fingertips through my puffed dough.

How good would I be if Homes filled me with a bit of his pimento cream?

"Oh...!" I dig my fingers deeper until my fingertips brush the cheesy hollow inside me. I squeeze my eyes shut and imagine Homes's smiling face between my thighs.

A disjointed fantasy dances through my fevered mind. What would it be like with him? Would he fill me to bursting, or would I end up trying to stuff myself through the hole in his bagel?

Does it matter?

What I can't stop picturing is what it would be like to fall into bed with someone who doesn't tell me that I taste exotic, or complain about my ingredients, or ask why I'm always in the same region of cuisine from one day to the next. What if Homes could like me... for me?

I finger myself until my dough loses all of its air, but I can't seem to find release. I'm too full of questions. I finally give up, lick the cheese off of my fingers, and reach for my phone. It takes me a minute to transfer Homes's number from the photo to my contacts. I'm not sure what to say, and I'm still hot and bothered from my earlier efforts.

In the end I just text, *Hi, it's Nat. Did I get the number right?*

Then I toss my phone onto the coffee table and get up. I need to do something, or I'll go crazy waiting for him to respond.

I grab my laptop, open a new tab in my browser, and start researching pop-up restaurants.

Chapter Four

I barely make it through the door after work before I collapse facedown on the carpet.

"Rough day?" Leftovers asks without looking away from the TV.

"I did it." Our carpet is old; I doubt the landlord has changed it in decades, and the smell is more than a little worrying. It's a sign of just how done I am that I can't even muster the gumption to lift my head.

"Did what, buddy?" Leftovers asks.

"I gave her my number."

For a moment, all I hear is the low babble of the TV, but then it goes silent. "Homestyle," Leftovers drawls, "I'm going to have to ask you to repeat yourself, because it *sounded* like you said that you finally made a move on dreamgirl."

"Nat," I mumble into the carpet. It smells faintly of stale bread and old milk. And... tuna? "You heard correctly."

"*Aww yeah!*" Leftovers leaps off the couch and starts doing an obnoxious hip-thrusting dance. No doubt we're going to get another noise complaint over this. "Go get it, go get it, that's my boy. Look at Homestyle, mac-n-cheesin' on the ladies!"

"Don't get too excited." I roll onto my back so that I won't have to keep puzzling over the tuna smell anymore. "I think she drank it."

Leftovers pauses. "You think she drank your number? Bro, are you baked?"

I explain the situation, including everything I overheard at the table afterward. "Her friend was saying all this TERB-y shit, and Nat didn't make a peep!"

Leftovers sinks down onto the sofa again. He's got that thoughtful expression on, the one I think of as his guru face. "Did she seem like she was agreeing?"

"I don't know. Her back was to me. And her other friend was responding, but... she didn't say a word." I press my palms to my eyes.

"Wellll..." Leftovers nibbles his lower lip thoughtfully. He doesn't look quite as stale today as he sometimes does. I seem to recall him telling me that he picked up a shift tonight. "I mean, that's not *great*. And personally, I'd like to see you with somebody who would actually stick up for you. But then again, she *had* just had someone come onto her a little strong. She might have been in shock."

"Could be, I guess," I murmur.

"And even if she drank your number, now she knows you're interested. Good job, Homesie. I'm proud of you."

I blow a raspberry at the ceiling. "You don't have to tease me about it."

"I wasn't." I'm used to sarcastic Leftovers, but right now, he sounds totally sincere. "I've seen you thirst after people before, but I've *never* seen you make a move."

"But that's because—"

"Because you don't think it's possible for the people you like to like you back. You think everyone's out of your league, Homesie. Fun fact? This chick would be lucky to have you. I guarantee you'd be more fun to be around than some snotty TERB, anyway."

"Thanks." I sigh and let my eyes drift shut. "I appreciate the sentiment."

Something buzzes against the carpet. In the throes of my histrionics, my phone slipped out of my pocket. I lift my head in a halfhearted effort to see the screen. The preview shows only an unknown number and the words: *Hi, it's Nat. Did I...*

"WHAT!?" I shriek as I reach for my phone.

Before I can pick it up and get the screen open, Leftovers tackles me and yanks the phone out of my hands.

"No!" he says, shaking a warning finger in my face. "Absolutely not. You *cannot open that chat* until you have a plan."

"What? Why?" I wriggle around beneath him and try to snatch my phone back. "Give it here!"

Leftovers presses his stale-pizza body against mine and holds the phone out of reach, way over my head. Curse my short, doughy arms.

"The minute you open that text, it's going to show up as *read*. She'll know you looked at it instantly and then took forever to reply!"

"I won't!" I whine as I try to grab it back.

Leftovers squirms around until he's sitting on my chest. "Yeah? Okay, what are you going to do if she's like, *Thanks but no thanks?*"

I thrash to one side and then the other. "Cry myself to sleep, quit my job, change my name, and move to Toledo. See? I have a plan."

"And what," he asks, "if she wants to meet up?"

I flop back on the carpet. "Um... I... wow." My plan pretty much began and ended with giving her my number. It was a way to make a move without seeming like I was *making a move,* but my roommate has a point. I have zero chill and even less game.

Leftovers smirks down at me. "That's what I thought. Fortunately, I'm here to help."

"Oh, thank God." I flick his arm. "Leftovers to the rescue. When was the last time you went on a date again?"

He pokes my forehead. "Rude. Do you want my help or not?"

I'm not sure that I want his particular brand of assistance, but my alternative is winging it on my own. Clearly, I need *someone* to help me out here, and Leftovers may well be my only hope.

"Fine," I grunt.

He lifts one eyebrow. "How about, *Thank you so much, I value your assistance?*"

"Thank you, you're the best, I don't know what I would ever do without you. Now, will you *please* let me read the text?"

"Nope." He opens my screen and stays put. "But I'll read it to you. I don't think you can be trusted with this right now."

"It's *my* phone, she messaged *me...*"

He ignores me and reads the text aloud. "*Hi, it's Nat. Did I get the number right?* Okay, not bad. Not too warm, either, but that's understandable. What do *you* think we should say?"

"There's no *we*, it's just me," I retort. "And I would say, *Yes, it's me.*"

"And?" Leftovers prompts.

"*I wasn't sure you would text?*" I frown. "No, that's too wishy-washy. Maybe it would be better to ask how her night's going?"

Leftovers nods. "Better. Engage with her. Don't just talk *at* her."

I blow another raspberry at him. "See? I can do this myself."

Leftovers wipes the berry juice off of his cheek disdainfully. "Maybe, but if I'd left the phone with you, you'd have instinctively sent your first answer and then gone, *Why did I say it that way?* and proceeded to have a meltdown about it. Tell me I'm wrong."

"You're... not wrong," I grumble.

Leftovers smirks and types on the phone, while saying aloud, "*Yes, it's me. I'm glad you messaged. What are you doing tonight?*" He glances up. "Are you good with me sending this?"

I roll my eyes. "Do I really get a say?"

"Dude, I'm not gonna be your Cyrano de Burgerac. I'm just your, like..." Leftovers purses his lips as he stares down at me for a moment. "Your filter."

"Send it," I say.

He does, then he holds the phone close to his chest while he talks to me. "So what's the plan? Flirt? Ask her out?"

"Ask her out?" My chest is already compressed from Leftovers sitting on me, but if it wasn't, the idea of asking dreamgirl on a date would knock the wind right out of me. There's one immediate problem, however. "How can I ask her out? I don't *go* anywhere."

"So figure out a new place to take her." Leftovers shakes his head incredulously. "It's not hard, man. We've got the *whole internet* at our fingertips."

The phone vibrates.

"What did she say?" I wheeze.

Leftovers reads the text and sucks in a breath. "Holy shit."

"*What!?*"

Leftovers can't tear his eyes away from the screen. "We have a situation."

I thrash again. "You're doing this on purpose!"

My roommate shakes his head. "I swear I'm not. But listen to this: *Figuring out my plans for the weekend. You?*"

I go limp again. "Do you think she's, um..." I stare at the ceiling in shock. "Do you think she's suggesting...?"

"Oh, she wants you. She's giving you an opening." Leftovers licks his lips. "You gotta be careful here. Chicks are squirrely. One wrong word, and they'll ghost."

I've been still long enough to lull Leftovers into a false sense of security. While his guard is down, I roll sharply to one side. He squawks in alarm and pinwheels his arms, but it's too late. He lands cheese-down on the carpet, and my phone goes flying. Before he can get to his feet, I scoop my phone up and bolt for my room.

"Ingrate!" Leftovers howls.

"Sorry-not-sorry!" I fire back as I slam my door and lock it behind me. I sit down with my back to the wood and open the chat again.

Somehow, one of us not only managed to hit a bunch of random keys during the scuffle, but also managed to hit send. I groan when I see that the second text I've ever sent Nat is *jkklaffksjvnm.*

I take a deep breath. I can come back from this. I'm still considering what to send when my phone buzzes.

Sounds exciting. 😁

I snort as I tap out a reply. *Sorry, I dropped my phone. Any exciting plans so far?*

Nat: Not yet. I don't get out much.
Nat: How about you?

Leftovers is right. Dreamgirl is giving me an opening. All I need to do is ask her.

Only, I have no idea what to ask her *to.*

Well, crap.

"Heyyyy, buddy?" I call as I unlock the door.

Leftovers is already curled up on the couch again, watching his show. There's lint stuck to his crust. When I sidle over to him, he flips me the bird.

"Let me guess," he grunts. "You need my help now."

"I'm just wondering, hypothetically, if you were going to take a girl on a date..." I wheedle.

Leftovers rolls his eyes.

"Aw, come on, Lefty." I jostle him with my elbow.

"Don't," he grunts. "I'm still mad at you."

"But I need your help." I bat my eyelashes at him and snuggle closer. "Come on, ol' buddy. Ol' pal. Friendo. Help a guy out."

Leftovers glares at me. "Why should I?"

"I'll grovel?" I suggest.

"It's too late for that."

"I'll clean the kitchen."

He snorts and turns back to the TV. "It's your turn anyway."

"Aw, come on, Lefty. Please?" I clutch my phone in both hands. "I'm sorry I flipped you."

"It's not about the flip," he grunts. "It's about trust." He sizes me up out of the corner of his eye. "Oh my *God,* stop looking at me like I just stepped on your pet hamster. It's sad." He whips out his phone and pulls up something in his email. My phone buzzes a second later with a new message from him. It's a screenshot of the ad for a show at a bar in town.

"It's a public place," he says. "Ask her out for a drink. Tell her that the drummer is a friend of a friend."

"Thank you!" I squeeze Leftovers in a one-armed hug. "You're a lifesaver."

"Remember that," he warns. "Now leave me alone."

"You know," I say, "Nat comes into the shop all the time with her friend. I could ask if they both want to go? If you're free Saturday, I mean?"

Leftovers kicks his feet up on the coffee table. "You want me to be your wingman, huh? This friend. Is she one of the ones who was giving you shit today?"

I wince. "Yeah..."

"Ask her to join," Leftovers says. "I'd love to give her a piece of my mind."

"Lefty!" I whine.

"I'll play nice if she will. Now shoo. I'm going to have to rewind this whole episode, Homesie." He shoves me off the couch, and I scurry back to my room to plan my next message.

Me: Actually, my friend and I are going to a show.
  Me: [1 attached image]
  Me: If you still don't have any plans, maybe you'd like to join me?

I hold my breath, waiting for her reply. One minute ticks by. Two. Every moment is its own private agony.

After ten minutes or so, I give up and throw caution to the winds.

Me: It wouldn't have to be a date. You could invite your friend.
Me: I'd like to get to know you better.

After they're sent, I reread my texts obsessively. Good lord, I sound pathetic. Leftovers was right about my palpable desperation and my resulting spiral. I should have let him handle things.

The rest of the night passes without a response. I end up lying facedown on my pillow, smushing my nose into its plush folds, wishing that the universe would take pity on me and just let me quietly smother.

If I were Nat, I wouldn't respond to me, either.

Chapter Five

"Wow." India leans on the prep table and lets her eyes sweep over me. "Rough night?"

I can't blame her for asking. Today, I'm an egg. A hardboiled egg. No salt, no seasoning. I'm not even peeled. I'm *never* eggs, but when I rolled out of bed this morning I thought, *Fuck it,* and didn't bother changing before I came to work.

"I'm assuming I look like shit," I grumble.

"Could be worse. Could be plain toast." India squints at me. She has no room to talk; she's a spicy little *mirchi vada* this morning, and as usual, I'm tempted to ask for her recipe. "Do you want to talk about it?"

"I'm cooking," I say, shooing her away with the spatula. I hate being a hardboiled egg. My shell doesn't fit properly over my white, and I've been sweating ever since I arrived.

India reluctantly leaves me to it, but when the restaurant finally closes, she and Monty ambush me by the register.

"We need to talk, boss," Monty says stoically.

I try to slip around them. "I'm fine, you two. Seriously."

"That's BS and you know it." India follows me, doing a body block so that I'm trapped behind the L-shaped counter. She's not terribly substantial, but she's got Monty at her back, and I don't think I could take him in a fight even if I had the energy for a rumble.

"We're worried about you," Monty adds.

I'd love to run checkout on the register, but I *do* kind of want to talk to someone about what's going on. Spilling my guts to my employees probably isn't the most professional course of action, but I don't know who else to confide in. My parents? Give me a break. Keto? I'm not sure I can confide in her after the way she was talking yesterday. At least India will understand.

"Someone asked me out last night," I blurt.

India and Monty exchange a skeptical glance.

"On a date?" India asks in a hesitant voice.

"Yes. Well, maybe not. He said it didn't have to be a date, but I think that was what he had in mind." I start stabbing the buttons on the POS with unnecessary force.

Monty clears his throat. "Is the lad in question particularly, erm, *unappealing?*"

"No. He's adorable, honestly." And awkward, too, but that's kind of cute. I don't mind a bit of awkwardness in a conversation. It puts me at ease, since it makes me feel like *I* don't have to try and be perfect all the time.

India nibbles a thumbnail as she examines me. "But you don't like him?"

"He seems fine." I run the sales for the day and scowl at the screen as the ticker-tape feeds out a spool of our records.

Monty adjusts his beans absently. "I'm sorry if I'm not understanding the problem, Nat. Perhaps we've missed something."

I press my palms to the counter and hunch my shoulders. Truth be told, I'm not sure how to put my concerns into words, even inside my own head. "I don't date," I mumble. "And if I did..."

India and Monty wait for my explanation with bated breath.

"I'm not sure I could date someone like him," I say. The words are barely out of my mouth, and I already feel gross. I still don't like Keto's attitude from yesterday, but I keep recalling how I felt when I walked down the street with her and Brunch. Like I was part of the in-crowd at last. I hate feeling like I don't belong anywhere—it's a feeling that's plagued me my whole life. When I was growing up, my mom was always after me to date boys from the Thai food community in her church. She never understood that I didn't belong there, either.

And yet, I keep wondering what Keto would think if I told her that I was going on a date with Homes.

"Why not?" India asks. Fortunately, she isn't privy to the maelstrom of thoughts swirling around my head.

The image of Homes's shy, smiling face pops into my head. Am I really going to let my anxiety about Keto's opinions influence me this much?

No, I decide. I'm not.

"I need you to finish closing up," I say. "Monty, do you mind counting the register?"

He shakes his head, although he's still watching me with that bemused, slack-jawed expression he adopted earlier.

I leave them to it, take my purse, and set off for the coffee shop at a trot. I want to talk to Homes *without* Keto for once.

I want to decide for myself how being around him makes me feel, rather than letting someone else decide for me.

There's one immediate bump in the road that I didn't anticipate: I usually only come here on Tuesdays, which is during Homes's usual shift. Wednesday, it seems, is not on his schedule. Instead, I'm greeted by a towering coffee cup of a woman who seems to be literally vibrating with excess caffeination. Block letters on her forehead spell out *Death Before Decaf.*

From a customer service perspective, it's a bit intimidating, but I admire the dedication.

"Hey-what-can-I-get-for-you?" she asks in such jittery staccato that I can barely make out individual words.

I can't tell if I'm speaking more slowly to calm her down, or if my regular speech just sounds strange by comparison. "I'm looking for Homes. Is he in today?"

"Homestyle?" She twists around toward the stockroom. "Yeah-I-think-so-he-was-just-here-but-let-me-go-check-his-shift's-almost-over-so-he-might-be-gone-already." She bolts away and throws open the stock room door.

I'm starting to wonder if that tattoo might be literal. One more shot of espresso, and the woman might need medical treatment. I vaguely recognize her from somewhere, which strikes me as odd, because she doesn't seem like the sort of person one would *forget*.

When she reemerges from the doorway, however, I manage to place her. She attends small-business mixers sometimes, although I don't think I've ever spoken to her directly.

How many other people have I failed to engage with just because Keto doesn't give them the time of day?

"He'll-be-out-in-two-seconds-he's-just-finishing-up," the woman says. "Can-I-get-you-anything-while-you-wait?"

"Actually, I'd like to introduce myself." I hold out a hand. "I think we've met before, but I forget your name. I'm International Fusion."

"Oh-you're-the-owner-of-Pig-in-a-Poke!" The owner of The Daily Grind extends one hand to me. She's shaking so badly that it takes me two tries to press my palm to hers. "I'm-Jo-nice-to-meet-you."

We're interrupted by a clatter. Homes has emerged from the stockroom carrying an armload of baking supplies, and two small containers of baking soda now lie on the floor where he dropped them.

"Nat," he gulps. His eyes dart from me to Jo and back. "You're... here." He's little more than a slice of sourdough toast. I wonder how much of that is my fault. I shouldn't have ghosted him last night.

"Yeah, I... I was hoping we could talk." I wipe a few beads of cold sweat off of my shell. "But if now's not a good time—"

"Now's fine," he interrupts. "Just let me finish stocking."

Homes bends to pick up one of the canisters of baking soda, and I kneel to retrieve the other. I make damn sure that our hands don't touch when I return it to him. The last thing I need is for sparks to fly between us. Cooking is just chemistry, and I'm not ready to find out how my ingredients react to his. Not until I can get my head on straight.

Jo watches as Homes slips around behind the counter and kneels to stock the baking cart. When she's sure that he's occupied, she gestures sharply to me and leans over the counter, nearly spilling on me in her haste. In the slowest, most coherent voice she's used since I arrived, she whispers, "If you're going to break his heart, you damn well better do it gently."

Her words catch me off guard, in part because her tone makes it sound like a request rather than an order. She sounds almost... protective.

I'm not sure that I have anyone in my life who feels that way toward me. Monty, maybe? India? They care about me, but they're my employees. It's not hard to imagine Keto threatening to break a few eggs if someone I liked hurt my feelings, but she hurts me all the time without even realizing it.

I realize that the silence has stretched uncomfortably long, so I force myself to nod. "Yeah. Okay, yes, I promise."

Jo nods and rights herself again, just as Homes stands up from beneath the counter and dusts off his knees.

"Do you want to talk here?" He gestures toward the window. "At your usual table?"

I glance from him to Jo. "Sure," I say. "That would be fine." It's not like I have a better place in mind, and depending on how this conversation goes, it's nice to know that there will be someone who cares about Homes here to support him.

Homes nods to his boss, and we wander over to our window seat. Only then does it occur to me that, while we'll be hard to overhear, anyone walking by will see us. I think of Keto's comments from the day before, and my own anxiety about fitting in, and I scowl down at the tabletop.

People suck. And I'm including myself in that statement.

Homes slides into his chair and gestures for me to sit across from him. "I'm pretty sure I know what you're going to say," he mutters. "And you could totally do it in a text, you know. It would fine."

He looks so glum that I feel guilty all over again. Why am I acting like this? Yesterday, I was squeaking my cheese curds to the thought of kissing him. He's attractive, and polite, and I barely know him. Which is the usual reason people agree to go on dates with each other, is it not? To find out if the chemistry of attraction translates into something in real life?

I hang my purse on the back of the chair and take my time settling into my seat.

"I'm actually not sure I *could* do this through text," I say. I wasn't sure what we were going to talk about when I first showed up, but now that I'm here across from him, I'm finding it easier to make sense of my own feelings. Keto's voice, and my parent's judgments, and my own insecurities fade away, leaving only one question behind. "Why me?"

Homes blinks a few times. "Huh?"

"Why me?" I repeat. "Do you hit on a bunch of your customers, and I've just happened to catch your eye this time around?"

"No!" Homes reels back. "No, it's not like that. I don't flirt with people, usually. You're just... different."

My yolk sinks. I've spent most of my life feeling different. *You're so exotic, Nat. You're so pretty, Nat. You stand out in a crowd, Nat. I bet you don't taste like anyone I've met before. Where are you from? No, where are you really from? How long have you been here?* I've heard it all.

Homes's cheeks darken as he toasts under my gaze. "Trust me, even my roommate knows about you. It took me *months* to even get brave enough to ask your name. I know you're out of my league, and it was probably stupid, and I overstepped. I'm sorry. I promise I won't make it weird for you if you want to keep coming here."

I interlace my fingers and clench my hands together. "What

did you tell your roommate about me?" Once again, I brace for the usual answers: *That you're quite the dish. That I'd love to sink my teeth into a spicy little meal like you. That I like to try something now and then.*

Homes squirms and picks at his crust. "Um... gosh, it's going to sound so stupid."

"Try me."

"That you're my dreamgirl," he mutters.

Just what I thought. A dreamgirl. And the thing about dreams is that you wake up from them. Back before I gave up on dating, I heard the same story over and over. All of the guys I dated said the same thing sooner or later: I was a good spread, but I'm not the sort of meal you take home to family gatherings. Their parents can't handle exotic spices. I'm an acquired taste.

Homes drums his knuckles on the table, still lost in his own thoughts. "Sorry, I'm not very good at this. And I get that you aren't interested, but I just thought..." He swallows hard, then he lifts his eyes to mine while keeping his chin tucked down. "You know, a lot of people look at me like I don't fit. It makes me feel, I dunno. Small. But then you come in, and you're different, too, but you don't try to hide it. Like, you could be an egg all the time, if you wanted. You could blend in. But some days you do and some days you don't. You're just yourself, and that's beautiful."

I sit back in my chair, caught off guard by his phrasing. "What?"

"Oh, geeze." He presses his palms to his eyes. "Sorry, I said it was going to sound stupid!"

I blink at him a few times. *You're different, too.* Nobody's ever said anything like that to me before, and it hits hard.

"It's not stupid," I murmur.

Homes looks up to meet my eyes properly for the first time since I arrived. "It's not?"

I shake my head. Now that he's looking at me, I can't drag my eyes away. "It makes sense, but I think you're giving me too much credit."

Homes shrugs. "Agree to disagree."

I entwine my fingers. How many people have said the same kinds of things to Homes that they've said to me? The flattery doesn't do much for me, in part because I'm so sure that he's off-base with those comments, and talk is cheap. It's the idea that he might actually *get* me that makes me second-guess myself.

"I don't date," I blurt.

Homes winces. "Oh, shit, my bad. Are you ace or aro? Sorry, I wasn't thinking—"

I shake my head. "You apologize a lot."

"Sorry," Homes says, and then winces again.

"Don't be. And I don't mean that it's a hard and fast rule. I just mean that I'm out of practice, and I'm not sure that I want to get back *in* practice." I trace an abstract pattern on the table with my finger, making sure that I mean what I'm about to say. "Hypothetically, if a friend and I came to the show this weekend, could it be like... like Schroedinger's date? Could we decide if it's a date when we're there? I'm not looking for a relationship, but who knows. You might surprise me again." I offer him a shy smile.

Homes looks as if he's just been struck upside the head with a pickled herring. "Um. Yeah. Yes! Yes, definitely."

"Then let me ask a friend, and I'll let you know." I'm not comfortable going out to a place I don't know with two strangers, and besides, I want to talk to Keto about this. I want to challenge her idea of me, and perhaps more importantly, I want to see how she responds. If she can't learn to get over her preconceptions, do I even want to be her friend anymore?

"Okay, great." Homes beams at me. I can see why Jo feels so protective of him. He's unguarded. It makes me want to take him by the shoulders and shake him and tell him to mask his feelings better, or else someone's going to hurt him so badly that he won't bounce back.

God, I really hope I'm not the one who does it.

I get to my feet and retrieve my purse. "I'll be in touch. Thanks for talking." I hover by the table for a moment, wondering what else to say, before bolting for the door. On my way past the window outside, Homes waves to me, as happy as I've ever seen him. He's too cute for his own good. Or mine, for that matter.

Instead of heading home or checking in to make sure that Monty and India have finished up—something that they could do in their sleep at this point—I fish my phone out of my purse and type out a quick message to Keto.

Are you free? I have something I'd like to ask you.

Keto sits back against the arm of her sofa and stares at me. "You actually texted him?"

"I sure did." I try to relax, although there's something about Keto's apartment that makes it hard for me to unwind. It's mostly white, from the walls to the furniture, very mid-century modern and *deeply* unsettling. I'm always convinced that I'm going to spill something on the carpet.

Keto stares at me, shaking her head. "Wow. That's shocking, frankly."

"Why?" I demand.

"Nat, I have *never once* seen you show interest in another person. Not romantic interest, anyway. Hell yes, I'd like a front row seat to whatever happens on Saturday. Do we need, like, a code for if you're planning to go back to his place? Or a hand signal if you need me to get us out of there? Gosh, this is so exciting. I haven't been a wingwoman since college." She claps her hands in delight. "Can I tell Brunch? Or is this secret?"

"I... guess." I blink a few times. "To be honest, I'm surprised you're this excited about it. I kind of got the impression that you didn't approve of him."

Keto lifts one shoulder. "I won't say I'm not surprised. It seems like kind of a weird match, to be honest. You're an entrepreneur, he's a part-timer. You're all, like, driven and visionary and whatnot, and he seems content pulling coffees. Plus there's the whole, you know, *he used to be a dinner* thing. But it's not my job to judge." Her eyes pop wide, and she leans over to grasp my shoulders. "You know what this means, though."

"Er. Do I?" I'm still reeling from the fact that Keto's way more chill about all this than expected.

"Girl." Keto's breathing deepens to an almost sensual panting. "*Makeover*."

My eye twitches, but I don't argue. It's a small price to pay, all things considered, and who knows. Both Homes and Keto have already surprised me today.

Maybe I'll surprise myself, too.

Chapter Six

Leftovers thumps his fist on my bedroom door about an hour before we're supposed to leave on Saturday. "Come out. I want to see you."

I hide behind the door. "Why?"

"Because I know you're in there overthinking this, and I want to save you before you show up looking like you tried way too hard."

"I resent that remark," I grumble, but he's right. I've been in here overthinking this all day. Maybe it's a good idea to get a second opinion.

When I open the door, Leftovers moans. "Dude, what's all this?"

"Is it too much?" I was having trouble deciding what to be tonight, so I just went with a little bit of everything: a Scandinavian-style open-faced egg-on-black-bread sandwich, sausage, bacon, a fruit cup, orange juice *and* coffee, cottage cheese, and a sweet roll.

"Too much? Dude, you're like a one-man breakfast buffet." He shoulders past me and perches on the edge of the bed, then he examines me critically while tapping one finger against his pursed, judgmental pizza lips. "Okay, explain the thinking behind this."

I look down at myself. "She told me that we'll see if it's a date, right? So I figure, if I'm a little bit of everything, maybe she'll find something she likes."

I expect Leftovers to start critiquing, but instead, he just stares at me, taking me in.

"Okay," he says at last. "Let's say she finds something in all this she likes. What happens then?"

"You mean, like, kissing?" I squeak. I sound like a goddamn teenager. Not long ago, I was rubbing one out to the idea of Nat in my bed, but now that it's not a total fantasy and could theoretically *happen,* the mere thought of carrying on a conversation with her is enough to give me a panic attack.

Leftovers wrinkles his nose. "Nah, that's whatever. For the sake of argument, let's say she sees you like this, and she decides she wants a sweet, sweet dose of that good Vitamin D. She comes back here, swallows your meat, the whole nine yards."

My coffee bubbles at the very idea.

Leftovers holds up a warning hand. "Settle down, Guy Hungry. Let's say she chomps your pork belly. What then? Are you just gonna be bacon for the rest of your life?"

"No," I say, although I totally would if that's what it took to make her like me.

"Bullshit." Leftovers waves one hand at me. "I'm not saying that your idea couldn't work. If you want to seal the deal tonight, sure. If you want to keep her coming back for seconds for a few weeks, maybe. But have a little love for yourself, Homestyle. How about instead of letting her decide what to order off the menu, you just be yourself and see if that's enough to make her mouth water?"

I flop down on the mattress beside him and stare at the ceiling. "I hear you, Lefty. But what if I'm myself, and she doesn't like me?"

"Then she's not the one for you, bro." Leftovers shakes his head. "I'm not going to tell you how to live your life. All I'm saying is that I know you're a cool guy, and I hope she can see that, too. I watched you bend over backward trying to be the person your parents wanted you to be for *years*, and I saw how miserable that made you. I'd hate to see you put yourself through that again."

I sniffle twice.

"Homes, are you crying?"

"No." I punch him in the arm as hard as I can. "*You're* crying."

Leftovers tackles me and gives me some hardcore noogies while I screech and flail and try to poke him in the armpit, which he *hates*. By the time I call uncle, he's spilled half my OJ, smashed the mango in my fruit cup to a pulp, and gotten cat hair in my open-faced sandwich. We don't even *have* a cat.

He leaves me to get changed, and after a fair bit of consideration, I reemerge as a fruit-and-muesli-topped açaí bowl, with a chia seed garnish for good measure. It's not the sort of thing I'd be on a work day, and I don't go out much, but it's also *me*: colorful, sweet, toeing the line between mainstream and basic bitch, and unapologetically breakfast.

Leftovers meets me in the living room. I whistle when I see him, admiring his turkey and cranberry sauce sandwich. "Looking sharp, bud. Although you're a *little* out of season, aren't you?"

"Fuck you," Leftovers says amiably. "I'm not trying to make the cover of *Bon Appétit*. Besides, you don't want me unleashing too much of my raw sexual magnetism on your girl. She might decide to upgrade." He pops his sourdough collar.

Leftovers can be a handful, but I'm well aware that I'm lucky to have him in my life. He's the most supportive friend I could ask for.

Which doesn't stop me from giving him the finger as I stroll toward the door.

· · ·

The moment I see Nat, I swear my soul leaves my body. She's waiting by the door of the club, next to a spinach and egg white omelet I recognize as Keto. Nat is a perfectly steamed bun with a lovely egg wash, but her dough is saturated with rich purple. Other than a bit of powdered sugar sprinkled over her dome, she's kept her look simple, but I can tell that if I bit into her, she'd be light and airy all the way through.

She lifts one hand in greeting, but I can tell from her expression that she's not sure how I'll respond.

"Hey," I say as Leftovers and I approach. "Ladies, I'd like to introduce my best friend, Leftovers. Leftovers, this is Nat and Keto."

Nat shakes Lefty's hand, but Keto just looks him up and down before turning to her friend. "Shall we?"

"Wow," Leftovers said. "You were right about her."

Keto bristles and glares at him. "Excuse me?"

Lefty produces four tickets from somewhere on his person. "I said we should grab a booth before the place fills up." He offers her one arm, and after a brief hesitation, Keto takes it and lets him lead her inside.

"Sorry about him," I whisper to Nat. "He's always like that."

To my relief, she chuckles. "So is she. At the very least, I can promise that this won't be a boring evening."

I follow Leftovers's lead and offer her my arm. "You look great tonight, by the way. Ube milk bun, right?"

"Ube and coconut," she corrects with a grin. "And look, we match!" She gestures from my açaí base to her ube puff crust.

That seems like a good sign—not the coincidence so much as the fact that she pointed it out. I'm probably overthinking this, but why would she point out the parallel if she wasn't at least giving me a chance?

We find a booth at the back of the bar and settle in. Leftovers says something to Keto, and she scowls at him, but it's already so loud that I can't make out all the words.

Nat twists around in the booth to face me and cups her hand

around her mouth so that I'll be sure to hear her. "Maybe bringing them was a bad idea. Keto's a little, uh, opinionated?"

At least she knows it. The comment reminds me of what I overheard in the coffee shop the day I asked her out, and I wonder why Nat would hang out with someone who makes a habit of putting other people down.

"Don't worry about Leftovers, he can hold his own," I assure her. "And if nothing else, they'll make our not-a-date look better by comparison."

Nat laughs, which feels like another good omen. She's more relaxed today. I'm wound tighter than ever, but only because I've spent the latter half of the week hoping so desperately to make a good impression.

A server comes around to take our drink orders, and before he leaves, I slip him my card and tell him to leave the tab open. I make decent tips at the shop most days; I can afford to cover everyone for the night.

Nat slides over to me so that her shoulder brushes mine. I know that she's just trying to be heard over the milling crowd, but it still makes my heart skip a beat.

"So, Homes." Her smile is warm and teasing. Dammit, she's lovely. "If you *were* going to go on a date with someone, what would you want them to know about you?"

I swivel to face her more directly. Across from us, Leftovers and Keto are already squabbling about something.

"I'm not sure how much there is to know. My life's fairly simple. By design. You already know where I work, and Leftovers is pretty much my only friend outside of that." It sounds pathetic when I put it that way, but Nat doesn't seem put off.

"How long have you known each other?"

"Oh, geeze, *forever.* Like, pre-K. He was my neighbor growing up, and he spent a lot of time at our house, since his family's a little..." I wave one hand back and forth. Talking about childhood is tricky, because I know that it will eventually lead to questions about myself that aren't necessarily first-date conversation starters.

"What about your family?" she asks.

My stomach sinks. "They're also *meh*, but for different reasons."

Our waiter returns with a light beer for Lefty, a vodka cranberry for Keto, a hard cider for me, and an over-the-top cocktail with a little umbrella for Nat.

"What the hell is that?" Leftovers shouts to her.

Nat grins at him. "Sex on the beach." Her eyes dart my way as she wraps her lips around the straw and takes a sip.

Ho. Ly. Shit.

Leftovers holds his hand out for a high-five, and Nat slaps it, while Keto looks on in disapproval.

Nat turns her attention back to me. Her smile fades a little. "I get what you mean about family being *meh*. My parents and I aren't really on the same wavelength, either. I'm still sorry to hear it, though."

I take a gulp of my cider. "Yeah, well. It is what it is. When I came out, they were... I dunno. I guess they don't approve." Might as well rip this Band-Aid off now, so I add, "You know I'm DtB, right?"

Nat nods as she swirls her curly straw through her drink. "Yeah. I did a little research about that the other night, actually. Hey, can I ask you something? You don't have to answer if you don't want, of course. I'm just curious."

I sip my cider again and brace for impact. "Bring it on."

"How did you know?" Nat frowns at me. Our eyes meet, and for a moment, I forget that there's anyone else in the bar with us. It feels like we're in our own private world. "I'm assuming that you'd had people telling you your whole life what you were, and who you were, and what that meant. How did you know that they were wrong?"

Of all the questions I'm prepared for, this isn't it. I'm struck once again by the fact that nobody else looks at me quite the same way she does, not even Leftovers. Like she *sees* me.

"That wasn't the hard part," I admit. "I knew for as long as I can remember."

"So what *was* the hard part? Telling people?"

I shake my head. "Admitting it to myself. I kept fighting it, telling myself that it was just a phase and that it would go away, or I'd grow out of it, or that I was just curious, but... it didn't change. And at some point, I finally realized that I needed to learn to live my truth, or the lie was going to kill me." I squeeze my eyes shut and pinch the bridge of my nose. "Aaaaaand now I sound like some frickin' fortune cookie. Want me to tell you your lucky numbers while I'm at it? Or teach you how to say *'socially awkward'* in Mandarin?"

Nat smiles, but she doesn't let me change the topic. "It's hard to put big feelings into words," she says. "Earnestness is always awkward, right? Because it requires defying social norms, I mean." She shakes her head and slurps on her straw until she sucks air. "Ignore me. It's been so long since I flirted with anyone, I think that whole lobe of my brain has atrophied."

"*Are* you flirting with me?" I ask in delight.

"See?" Nat waves a hand at me. "You can't even tell! Go on, ask something about me."

She's right about that filter thing, because I don't stop to think before asking, "Why *don't* you date?"

Nat groans and rolls her eyes. "A series of shitty exes. Bad company, dull conversation, and disappointing sex. What's the point? Besides, I've been busy with the restaurant."

At the word *sex,* my face flares hot. I try to douse the sudden warmth in my belly with a liberal application of hard cider, but it doesn't help. "Sorry to hear that."

"Good news, though." She lays her hand over mine and lowers her voice. "So far, the company has been good, and the conversation is interesting. So you're already doing better than my last few dates."

My brain goes offline for a moment, and it only reboots when she pulls her hand away.

"Sorry," she mumbles. "I don't know what I'm doing. Like I said, I'm out of practice. Ignore me."

"No." My voice comes out a squeak. I clear my throat before

speaking again in my normal range. "No, it's good. I mean, if that's what you're looking for, I wouldn't say no."

Nat appraises me again. "I sort of assumed that you were angling for a hookup."

"I'm angling to get to know you better." This conversation has me all out of sorts. My berries ache to think that she might want me as badly as I want her. All my dirty thoughts from the other day come rushing back. Thank God she can't read minds.

"Be real, though." She nudges me with her shoulder. "If you had to choose right now between going home with me, or scheduling a second date and leaving at this exact moment, which would you do?"

"Second date," I say without hesitation. "It would give me something to look forward to."

Nat raises her eyebrows. "Good answer."

The set ends, and the quiet that follows is unexpected. For the first time, I can hear what Leftovers and Keto are saying.

Leftovers hooks his thumb at her. "Homestyle, can you believe that she's never seen *Ratatouille*?"

"It's a children's movie," Keto protests. "Besides, rats in a kitchen? *Très* yuck."

"Don't knock it until you've tried it," Leftovers warns.

Nat raises her eyebrows at me as if to ask, *Have they been arguing about an animated movie this whole time?*

Knowing Leftovers, it's entirely possible.

The waiter comes back around, cutting the movie debate short. "Can I get you another round?" he asks.

Nat leans over me, and her thigh presses against mine. "I'll have a climax."

Our server grins. "My pleasure."

"*I'll* have a blowjob," Leftovers says.

"Um, yeah." I sink a little lower in the seat. My banana is ripening by the second. "Me, too."

Keto crosses her arms. "You are all *so* immature."

"Aww, come on," Leftovers says. "You can drink your low-carb cocktail and feel superior, but let us have our fun."

Keto exhales through her nose, then flicks her eyes toward the waiter. "I'll have a buttery nipple," she says.

"*Yesssss!*" Leftovers drums both palms against the table. "That's what I'm *talking about.*"

The waiter leaves, and I turn to Keto. "I hope my buddy isn't giving you *too* hard a time."

She rolls her eyes, but she doesn't seem particularly annoyed. "It's fine. We've mostly been talking about movies and shows."

"We're both fans of *Entrée-You*!" Leftovers exclaims.

"It's one of the most popular shows on air," Keto points out. "It's not like we're both into some weird, nerdy niche thing. I bet you're into loads of freaky stuff."

"Like you wouldn't believe." Leftovers jiggles his eyebrows. "I could show you sometime."

Keto pretends to gag.

The server comes back with our drinks. A climax, it turns out, is a creamy almond-and-banana cocktail. We raise our glasses in a toast.

"Here's to introducing new friends to our niche, freaky interests!" Leftovers says.

The rest of us clink glasses, and three of us throw back our shots while Nat takes a deep draught of her cocktail. "Want to taste mine?" she asks me.

Leftovers coughs meaningfully as I take a small sip of the drink. The alcohol has loosened something inside of me—I've had just enough to feel warm and relaxed, but not enough to be more than pleasantly buzzed. I decide right then and there to cut myself off. If Nat has another drink, I'm not going to let things go any further tonight. I refuse to be *that guy.*

The music starts up again, and Leftovers gets to his feet. He holds out his hand and shouts something in Keto's general direction. When she scoots out of the booth with him, Lefty gives me a wink.

I don't deserve a friend like him.

Nat sips her cocktail again. She's come over all pensive, and I wonder if she's worried about being left alone with me. Then she seems to make up her mind about something and leans against me, pressing her mouth so close to my ear that I can feel her lips move.

"I don't know what dating looks like for me," she says. "I've been all over the map recently. But I haven't been able to stop thinking about what you said in the coffee shop the other day, and..." She takes a shaking breath. "And it has been a *really* long time since I got laid. Like, a *long* time. And I'd like to kiss you, if that's okay. Maybe more than kiss you. How would you feel about that?"

"Um. *Excellent.*" Shit, shit, shit. I want this, I really do, but I also have *no fucking clue* what I'm doing. "When?" I ask, stalling for time. I mean, come on, there's no way that I'm going to turn her down, but if I kiss her, I guarantee that she's going to *know*.

Her lips turn up in a smile. "Why not now? Nobody here is going to care."

True. And it's kind of nice to realize that she doesn't mind kissing me in public, in front of her TERB-y friend. I shift toward her, cupping one cheek with my palm and letting the other settle on her waist. I lean toward her, wondering how to go about this without doing something stupid like clacking my teeth against hers or smearing açaí all over her egg wash.

Nat solves the problem by wrapping one arm around my back and reaching up to run her fingers through my muesli. My eyes flutter shut at her caress, and the next moment, her lips meet mine.

Cooking produces a permanent chemical change in the ingredients' molecular structure. A baked potato can never become raw again. A steamed stalk of asparagus will never regain its natural crispness. The sugars and acids in a steak that has undergone the Maillard reaction will never reform.

And I will never again be the same person I was before I tasted International Cuisine.

Her mouth is warm and soft against my own, and her doughy middle gives beneath the press of my hand. She exhales hard and sharp before parting her lips and licking into my mouth. The savory-sweet flavor of ube bread mixes with my fruity base, leaving me dizzy with desire.

Beneath the table, my hand slides down to her thigh, and she freezes.

I pull away from her and lift my hand from her leg again. "Sorry."

Nat's eyes are starry and unfocused. "I think I need to get up."

"Yeah," I say. "Sure. If you need a moment alone, I totally understand—"

She nuzzles my jaw with her nose. "Not alone."

Oh. *Oh*.

I glance toward the dance floor. Leftovers is twerking like a maniac while Keto laughs her ass off at him. They look like they're having a good time. They're also so focused on each other that neither one of them notices when Nat slides out of the booth, takes my hand, and leads me away toward the bathrooms. She keeps hold of me even when she pokes her head into the women's restroom before dragging me into a stall. When she pulls me in for another kiss, I lean against her, settling my hips between her thighs.

"Shit," she breathes as she slides one hand under my shirt. "What is it about you? I don't normally do this, but..." Her eyes trace a lazy path from my stomach to my face. "Well, after all, you did order the blowjob."

I press my forehead to hers. "You don't have to."

She freezes again. "Don't you want to?"

I chuckle weakly as I roll my hips against hers. "I mean, obviously I want to. But if I had to choose, I'd still prefer that second date. I don't want to rush things."

Her fingers trace the curve of my spine from my lower back downward. "How about both?"

I suck in a breath. "Both is good."

"Good." She lowers her voice to a whisper. "Do you want to know a secret?"

"One of yours?" I ask. "Obviously."

Nat nips my earlobe. "I have an itty bitty hint of an oral fixation."

This can't be happening. I've died and gone to... heaven, I assume. Or maybe fun, kinky purgatory. When one of Nat's hands slides between us to trace the curve of my cooking implements, I moan.

"So what do you say?" she whispers.

"Yes. *Please.*" I'm not above begging, it seems.

Nat pushes me away from her, and I stumble back against the far wall. There's graffiti all over the walls in here, but at least it's cleaner than the guy's bathroom is bound to be.

By the time I realize what's happening, Nat's already on her knees in front of me, grinning up at me from waist-level as she fondles my equipment. When I changed earlier, I really didn't think that anything like this would happen. Nat meets my eyes as she takes my frosting nozzle in her mouth and fondles my aching açaí berries.

"Oh, *fuck.*" I have to brace my feet to keep from toppling over.

A dollop of glacé slips out of me, and Nat freezes. "Homes," she asks around a mouthful of candied fruit, "is this *cherry?*"

I'm going to die of embarrassment. "Yeah," I wheeze. "I'm not exactly smooth, in case you haven't noticed." In fact, I'm incredibly chunky. That first cherry almost clogged my nozzle, and there's more where that came from.

I should have told her that I was a virgin before she had my cherries in her mouth.

We stare at each other for a long moment as my nozzle starts to droop. Talk about embarrassing.

"Oh my God." She covers her mouth with one hand, looking absolutely mortified. "I'm so sorry. We could have taken things slower. Why didn't you say anything?"

I don't know what to tell her. *Because I didn't want you to think I was a loser.*

Because I didn't want you to be disappointed.

Because I didn't want you to stop.

Nat braces one hand against my thigh and the other against my belly. "Do you still want to do this?" she asks.

"Only if you do."

She takes me in her mouth again, but she's gentler this time, working her lips over my piping nozzle and her tongue over my star-tip. My eyes flutter closed, but I can still feel her watching me, gauging my reaction.

"Please don't stop," I whisper.

She keeps sucking me until my hips buck involuntarily.

"Sorry!" I squeak.

Nat pulls away and laughs, but her voice has turned low and husky. "I don't mind," she says. "In fact, if you wanted to do it a bit more, it would feel good."

I try doing what she suggests, moving slowly at first, and only a little. Soon enough, we fall into a rhythm, and the world spins around me.

"Is this all right?" I rasp.

Even the split-second that she pulls away is agony. "God, yes. Fill me, Homes. *Fill me.*" She slides her mouth over me again. When she groans, I groan with her.

This isn't anything like what I imagined.

It's better.

I thrust deep, releasing a more plentiful squirt of tart cherry filling, and Nat moans. It's hard to control myself, and a few times, a cherry gets stuck in my open star-tip, only to burst free along with a rush of acidic syrup. I try to fill her evenly, squeezing into her until she's swollen with my citrusy, piquant load.

The room spins when Nat finally pulls away. My piping tip slips out of her without warning. In my excitement, I drizzle a thin line of icing over her laminated crust by accident, and she gasps.

"Sorry," I pant. "I didn't meant to—"

Nat smiles up at me; she's taken so much of my internal produce that her cheeks are flushed. "No," she whispers. "I like it. I... I want you to frost all over me."

I can't believe this is happening. Nat keeps grinning up at me, and the fact that it's *her* is too much. An uneven zigzag of starch-thickened icing gushes out of me, accompanied by a lusty moan.

When the last surge of my passion splatters across Nat's egg-washed dome, I almost collapse.

"Sorry," I rasp. "I've never frosted before and... I made kind of a mess." My icing is already hardening on her flaky exterior. She looks so milky and soft, with a pull-apart texture that leaves my mouth watering all over again.

"Don't apologize." Nat gets up. She drags one finger through the frosting I've squirted all over her chin and smiles at me as she sucks her finger. The lewdness of it, the sensuality of it, fries my brain.

Which is why the next words out of my mouth are so totally beside the point. "Oh my *God,* our friends are going to know exactly what we did..." Leftovers is never going to let me live this down.

She helps me rearrange myself into a relatively decent state. "Homes. It's *fine.* I'll just text Keto that I'm not feeling well and dip out the back exit." Nat pulls out her phone, then she shows me the screen. "Look, no problem, see? Keto already left. I only live a few blocks from here. I can walk."

"Do you want me to walk you home?" I ask helplessly. Now that I'm coming back down from the high of cramming her to the brim with my fruit compote, I'm starting to panic. I should do something for her, right?

"I'll be fine," she assures me. "You should go back out to your friend."

I don't want her to go. I'm convinced that if we part like this, I'll never see her again. She must think I'm a total freak, losing my cherries in a public bathroom to a pastry I barely know. "Is it okay if I text you later? I can't believe I left you room temperature. I can make it up to you."

Nat leans against me to plant a cherry-scented kiss on my cheek, and I'm suddenly aware of the heat rolling off of her.

"Trust me," she purrs, "you've got me all hot and toasty. You'll *definitely* be hearing from me. Besides, we have a second date to plan, remember?" With that, she opens the stall door, pausing to glance at herself in the mirror before vanishing into the hallway. She doesn't even bother trying to wash off the already-set frosting.

In the end, I don't have to explain anything to Leftovers. He's already gone by the time I stumble out into the bar. The band is packing up their equipment, the crowd has begun to disperse, and when I try to pay the tab, the waiter hands me my card back and tells me that my friend already took care of it. I float home feeling giddy with bliss, but also...

Disappointed.

Whenever I've pictured Nat in my bed, I've also fantasized about falling asleep next to her and waking up beside her the next day. Instead, I end up crawling into bed alone.

At least I'll get to see her again. I just hope that she doesn't change her mind, knowing what she knows. I'm not experienced, but I'm sure that what I felt when I kissed her isn't ordinary. Otherwise, people would never be able to think about anything else.

I dream of purple yams and steamed dough and licking Nat between her tremulant thighs until she overflows with silky pandan cream.

Chapter Seven

I barely get any sleep that night. Who am I? I've *never* begged a near-stranger to pump me full of fruit filling in public, much less let *anyone* frost my crust like that. The worst part—or at least, the most *confusing* part—is how I end up lying awake for hours as Homes's hot cherry compote cools inside me. I'd do it again in a heartbeat. I'm already wondering when I'll see him again.

The fact that I've taken his cherries complicates everything. It makes me feel almost responsible for his experience, which is absurd. But still. His first time was in the bathroom of some downtown dive bar?

Not just his first time. His *only* time.

You could change that, says the devil on my shoulder. *You could call right now, and he'd come running. You could dip his tea bag, hard-boil his eggs, crisp his bacon, and stuff his toad in your hole to your heart's content.*

With those mental images dancing through my mind, it's a wonder that I ever manage to fall asleep.

. . .

I can't seem to shake that feeling of selfishness. As sometimes happens when I'm in a rare mood, my appearance and my emotions match. I look as *shellfish* as I'm feeling. One glance at my mirror on Sunday mornings reveals that I am an oyster on the half shell, swimming in a fragrant mixture of lemon juice and brine. Thank God I have another day off; I can't be at work when I'm like this. Between being a health nightmare *and* an allergen, I'd have to call in backup even if I was scheduled.

Once I'm up and about, I reach for my phone. Those two drinks must have hit me harder than I realized, because I'm *never* oysters, and I'm dangerously close to brunch territory. All the same, whenever I think of Homes, I can't help the wet, limpid quiver that passes through me. Everything about him brings my oven right up to temperature, no preheating required.

When I open my lock screen, I see a text from Homes that reads, *Good morning. Hope you slept well.*

After a moment's hesitation, I send him a quick text back: *Slept fine. How are you today?* I might be feeling conflicted as hell about our encounter last night, but I'm not going to be an ass.

After that, I pull up Keto's number and give her a call. She answers on the third ring.

"Girl, what the heck?" she demands. "You ditched me last night!"

"I did not," I retort. "I was still in the bar when I got your text."

Keto lets out a huff of disbelief. "I must have missed you, then. How did it go? Did you have fun?"

I smack my lips a few times. "Um…"

"Oh my gosh, you slept with him!" Keto shrieks. "Hold that thought. I'll be there in twenty minutes with smoothies."

In fact, only fourteen minutes elapse between when I hang up and when my front door bursts open to reveal my friend, clutching a green goddess smoothie in each hand and breathing hard.

"The elevator was too slow," she pants. "I took the stairs. The gossip couldn't wait. Now sit down and spill the cold-press."

I give her a somewhat abbreviated version of the evening's events in between slurps of smoothie. Some of her concoctions are on the iffy side, but this one is actually pretty tasty.

Keto sits at my kitchen table in silence until I'm finished, and even then, she doesn't speak up right away.

"How do you feel about all this?" she asks.

"*Super* conflicted." I drain the last of my liquid breakfast. "I thought it would be a friends-with-benefits thing, you know, a hookup? A situationship? Like, we'd fool around and I wouldn't be that invested and I could get it out of my system or something? But part of me wants to call him over right now and spend the day in bed with him."

Keto whistles. "That good, huh?"

I swirl the remains of my smoothie. "I don't know. It's more like, there's something about him that makes me want to be nice to him. He's so..." I don't know how to explain the feeling.

Keto drums her fingers on the desk. "Mmkay, listen, Nat. I like you. A *lot*. And if you want to ride the train to pound town with someone like him, I'm not going to judge. But dating? Really?"

Her tones make warning alarms go off in the back of my brain. "Do you mean because he was born a girl?" That stops me short. "Woah, wait. Does this make me a lesbian?" I wasn't even thinking about that last night, but I spiral out for a few seconds as I follow a runaway train of thought about what this means for my sexual orientation.

"Um, *no*." Keto pulls a disgusted face. "Transmen are men, Nat. Like, you could still be bi or whatever, I have no idea, but don't get all gross and transphobic on me. No, the weird part is that he used to be a *dinner*."

"You think? Because I've only ever seen him as a breakfast. We were talking about it a little last night." My eyes glaze over as I remember what he said about living his truth. Supposedly, he thinks I'm brave or outgoing based on how I present myself to the world, but the truth is, I'm still terrified to go against the norm, even when normalcy chafes.

"More power to you." Keto examines her fingernails. "Like I said, no judgment. I've noticed you've been kind of down lately, and it seems like being around Homes makes you happy. Which is whatever, y'know? So if you want to spend the day in bed with him, why not go for it?"

It's a good question, one that I don't have a ready answer to.

"Thanks," I say slowly. "For coming out last night, I mean, and swinging by this morning." With another shock of guilt, I realize that I've been so caught up in my own drama that I haven't been thinking about what's going on for her at all. "Did you have any fun, or was it a total drag?"

"A little." Keto adjusts the avocados on her sprouted spelt toast. "Leftovers is kind of a man-child, but at least he's respect-ful. I'm used to guys like that jostling me around, touching me at every opportunity, telling me to lighten up, pushing my boundaries..."

I lift my empty cup in a weary solidarity.

"But he's not like that, so yeah, I did have fun. I didn't feel like I had to be on guard the whole time. If you must know, it made me feel a little better about your guy, knowing that his best friend isn't a creep... at least as far as I know." She gets up from the table. "I've gotta jet, babe, I've got Pilates class in half an hour and a lunch date with my sister after that. Just make sure to give me the juicy details at our meetup next week." She plants air kisses on my cheeks before sailing out the door.

I've definitely misjudged Keto. One of these days, I'll have to find a way to make it up to her—not only to assuage my guilt, but to show her how much I value her friendship.

In the meantime, I check my phone to discover a thread of missed messages from Homes.

I'm good. Missing you.

Not in a desperate way. In a very suave way. Looking forward to date number two.

Which I hope is still a thing.

I mean, not that you owe me your time. I just like being around you.

OMG I sound like a stalker I'm so sorry.

I wish I could un-send texts. Please ignore all of these.

"What a dork," I murmur fondly, before tapping out a text of my own. *Yes, very suave. I'm not up for going out, but if you're free tonight, maybe we could hang out at my place?*

There's enough of a pause after I hit send that I make myself get up and start unloading the dishwasher. I don't panic-babble like Homes does, but I certainly get nervous. I think I took things too far last night—or at least too fast. I should have pumped the breaks. Only, the moment his mouth met mine, sense and reason went out the window. I needed more.

I can't remember the last time I trusted someone enough to feel that way around them.

My phone chimes, and I hurry back to the table to read Homes's reply.

Homes: I'm sorry! I'm at work! Maybe after...?
    Me: At your convenience. What time would be good for you?
    Homes: 5?
    Me: Sounds perfect.

I debate about inviting him to my home—inviting a guy over on the second date is how 99% of *Chopped!* episodes start—but in the end, I text him the address.

I spend the rest of the day obsessively cleaning, not only because I've been slacking on that front recently, but also because I need to do *something* or I'll go crazy waiting.

It's just hormones, I tell myself. *Shellfish is an aphrodisiac.*

But despite my general pessimism, this feels like the start of something, and I'm as anxious as Homes is not to come across as desperate and lonely, despite the fact that I very much am.

It's five fifteen when Homes finally knocks at my door. Usually I'd be annoyed about the time, since I'm a fan of precision, but

I've spent the last hour panicking over whether or not I should serve dinner. Would that be polite? Or would it be weird to serve dinner to someone who's DTB? Clearly, I need to educate myself further. I can't count how many times I've shared awkward meals with new people who think they're doing me a favor and "respecting my culture" by serving me Top Ramen or fried rice out of a pouch.

In the end, I don't make anything. We can get takeout if he wants.

When I open the door to a knock, I find myself face to face with an absolute cinnamon roll of a man. He's dripping with a spiced-sugar glaze that immediately reminds me of last night, and his swirl is studded with currants. How can he be so damn sweet?

He deserves better than a booty call.

"Hey, Nat," he says, grinning like a fool. "I brought you these."

I force my gaze downward to the small reusable shopping bag he's holding. "What's this?"

"Um, just something I got for you." He pulls the bag back. "Never mind, it's silly."

I tug the bag out of his hands and grin at him. "Come on, let me see." When I upend it onto the counter, half a dozen wrapped cheeses tumble out: Brie, Camembert, Gouda, Gorgonzola, Havarti, and Wensleydale. I turn them over before glancing back toward Homes, who is standing just inside the door, looking stickier than ever.

He smiles sheepishly. "I was going to bring you flours, but then I thought that was cheesy, so I skipped the middleman and... oh, my God." He scoots toward the door. "I'm sorry. I'm such a dork, I don't know what I was thinking. I can go if you want."

"Don't." I gather my cheeses and grin at him. "Stay. I'll just pop these in the fridge and we can do... something." Now it's my turn to be awkward. I barely know him. Other than what he does for a living, and the identity of his best friend, what have we talked about?

Nothing, because you were too busy guzzling from his nozzle.

"What would you like to do?" I ask. "Sorry, I didn't think this through. We could watch a show, if you want?"

Homes shifts from foot to foot. "Is that really what you *want* to do?" He seems amused, and I wonder if he's relieved to find that I'm as awkward as he is about all this.

I nod toward the couch. "In case you missed the memo, Netflix and chilling is a classic excuse to get cozy."

"Do we need an excuse?" He smiles shyly at me. "Look, Nat, I like you. A lot. And after last night, I…"

"Yes?" I breathe.

Homes steps forward and caresses my nacre with his buttery, enriched dough. "I was hoping you'd let me touch *you* this time."

I gesture down at myself. "I'm not exactly in top form today, sorry. And besides, you don't owe me anything."

Homes busts up laughing. At first, it's just a guffaw, but once he gets going, he can't seem to stop, and he ends up bent double and reeling with laughter, clutching the edge of the kitchen table for support.

"What?" I demand, even though his laughter is infectious.

"You really think," he wheezes, "that I feel like I *owe you*? Nat, you don't understand. I've been feeling guilty as hell every time I fantasize about you, or dream about you, or wish I could be lying next to you. You think that me asking permission to go down on you is something I'm doing out of *generosity*? Or *debt*? Dammit, you have no fucking clue."

I gesture toward my jiggling, uncooked body. "Yeah," I say drily. "Who could resist all this?"

Homes hiccups into silence. "You're serious. You really don't get it. I've been driving myself crazy over you for weeks. *Months.* I want you. Like this, like you were yesterday, like you were the day before and like you will be tomorrow. All the time. Every time. I want to know the sounds you make and the way you move and how you feel when you're… when you…" He gulps.

Half of me wants to reach for him and the other half wants to pull away. After a lifetime of habit, I do the latter, wrapping my arms around myself and licking my lips, unable to meet his gaze. "And what if that doesn't happen?"

Homes nods. "That's fine. If you don't want me to, say so, and we can give *Entrée-You* a fair shake instead. Netflix and Netflix, no chill required."

"That's not what I mean. It's hard to get my head in the right place sometimes. So what if we, uh, fool around, and nothing comes of it?" *Great word choice, Nat. Classy.*

Homes shrugs again. He's still smiling. "If you think I'm worried about how you'll *perform,* then you're missing the point, Nat."

I let out a raspy chuckle and point one finger accusingly at him. "Oh ho ho, you didn't warn me. You're *way* better at this than I am."

He blinks in surprise. "At what?"

"At flirting. Wow." I fan myself a little. "Yeah, I... yeah. Let's do whatever you have in mind."

This time, Homes is the one to take my hand and lead me to the couch. Instead of turning on the TV, however, he makes sure I'm settled, then kneels in front of me so that he's eye-level with my already dripping flesh. He kisses my thigh, then looks up at me.

"If you want to stop, say the word."

I shiver. "We're already off to a good start."

He gently traces the edge of my quivering muscle with his pastry tail, prying my limpid flesh away from the glistening shell below. I gasp, amazed at how sensitive I am already.

"Is that... good?" he asks, pausing while I answer.

A weak, "Uuuh..." is all I can manage.

Homes looks pleased with himself, and he touches me again gingerly. I'm left a trembling wreck within a matter of seconds. I pant out my desire, only just holding it together. My brine and lemon soak into him, swelling his pastry with my salty juices.

And then his hesitant caress brushes across my pearl.

"Oh, God." My voice snags in my throat, raw as the palpitating meat of my mantle.

Holmes chuckles.

"You're enjoying this too much," I groan.

"Yeah?" His pastry caresses my pearl again. "Is that so?"

I tremble as I glare up at him, trying to look fiercer than I am. "Stop messing around. Either touch me, or..."

His pastry encircles my pearl. His raisin has risen, and his walnuts nudge my flesh as he fondles himself, all while brushing across me in gentle strokes. "Like that?" he asks.

"More," I pant.

His pastry slides under me. He's getting soggy now, as my brine soaks into him. I don't know how much longer either of us can last. I don't want this to end, but I want more. I need more. I've been going out of my mind with desire all day, and I'm so close...

"Homes?" I pant.

"Yeah." His lips are slick with my juices. *He brought you cheeses,* I think wildly. *How can he be so sweet and clumsy one moment, and so filthy the next?*

"I want you... I need you to..." I can't say it.

His raisin nudges my pearl. "Tell me. Tell me what I can do for you, Nat, *please.*"

The word that emerges from me is more breath than speech. *"Swallow."*

His tongue darts out, licking my citrus brine from his lips as he pants against my pearl. Then he slides further beneath me, lifting me from the glistening bed of my shell. For a moment, I can't tell where his mouth stops and I begin.

His throat bobs, and I scream his name in sweet relief as he tips me back and swallows me whole.

Chapter Eight

It's Monday, and I'm sitting on the couch when Leftovers steps out of his room. At first, I barely glance up from the TV, but when I see him, my jaw drops. "Dude," I gasp, "who are you and what have you done with my friend?"

Leftovers flips me the bird, but he won't meet my eyes. "It's not a big deal."

"You're a fucking *chipped steak omelet* today," I point out. "This is the most effort you've made, like, *ever.* Shit, you're even wearing *garnishes.*"

Leftovers fusses with his scallions. "What's your point?"

My eyes widen as the implications of this sink in. "Lefty," I say slowly, "do you have a *date?*"

"Is it really that improbable?" he asks. I've never seen him this shy and defensive. He must really like whoever he's meeting up with if he's taking it this seriously.

I mute the TV. "I'm not making fun. I'm just curious. You know that you can tell me anything, right?"

His shoulders relax a little, and the ghost of a smile steals over his face. "It's nothing serious. I'm just meeting up with a friend." He wanders over to the couch and socks me in the shoulder. "Good luck with your family today, dude. If it gets too weird, just pretend I texted you that I'm in the hospital and need you to come bail me out."

"The hospital, or jail?" I ask skeptically. "I think you're mixing your metaphors."

"Po-tay-to, po-tah-to," Leftovers says airily. "Tell them I accidentally swallowed some dude's mixed nuts, and I'm having a severe allergic reaction. They'll believe that. Later, asshole!" He pauses by the mirror to adjust his scallions one last time and then heads out alone.

Truth be told, I should be getting ready, but I *hate* going home. I always struggle with whether I should avoid a fight by going as something that won't freak my parents out, or being myself. I tell myself it's no big deal. It's one afternoon. It'll be so much easier if I just go as a ham-and-cheese snack wrap, something innocuous that *could* be breakfast or *could* be dinner depending on your perspective.

Lefty's words from the other night have really stuck with me, though. Trying to please other people never got me anywhere, and it made me depressed as hell. I decide, fuck it, I'm gonna be me.

I go into my room and change into a smoked salmon eggs Benedict with dill hollandaise, then examine myself in the mirror.

Perfect. This is a good look for me. The Homes I see in the mirror and the Homes I see in my head are getting closer and closer to each other every day. By the time I leave, I'm actually smiling, and I *feel* it.

It's a sign of how far I've come.

Of course, it doesn't last. Good feelings *never* last in that house.

Mom is going through old photo albums when I arrive. She has them all laid out on the table, and she's poring over them with the sort of expression that tells me I'm walking into the middle of an argument. My sister, Diner, sits beside her. When she sees me, she shakes her head.

Great. Photo albums. Just what I wanted.

"Sit down, baby," Mom says. "We were just getting to the good stuff."

My sister rolls her eyes behind Mom's back. True to form, Mom is a lasagna today, while Diner is a gravy-smothered chicken-fried steak.

"Meat-and-Two-Veg!" Mom calls. "Your son is here! Come say hello!"

Yup, they're fighting. They only call each other by their first names when something's wrong.

Dad sways in from the living room. He's a hearty slice of meatloaf, a pile of mashed potatoes, and a mound of garlic-butter green beans. There's comfort in his familiarity, although I can't help but notice that his portions have gotten bigger lately.

"Hey, Homes," he grunts. "How's it hanging?"

I open my mouth to reply, but Mom cuts me off. "Homestyle, have you heard about Jel?"

Diner groans. "Let it go, Mom."

Mom ignores her. She clasps her hands on the table in front of her and adopts a stiff smile. "Jel is your father's new secretary. She's your sister's age."

"She's just a temp, Talia." My father yanks open the door of the fridge and fishes out a beer. "You want one, Homes?"

"Don't pretend you hired her for anything other than her jiggle, Meaty." Mom's smile turns as poisonous as a destroying angel.

"I *hired* her because nobody else knows how to work the spreadsheets, and she's got good people skills."

"Oh, I bet she does," Mom mutters.

"Jealousy isn't a good look for you, honey." Dad pops the top off of his beer and lumbers back to the living room.

"Wow," Diner says brightly, "this is fun. I'm glad I came. Aren't you glad you came, Homes?"

I hastily turn to the open album. "What are we looking at?"

Mom sniffs. "Our wedding pictures. Back when your father

agreed to love me *for better or for worse, until death do us part!*" She bellows the last words at the top of her lungs.

From the next room, my dad retorts, "And I've prayed for an act of God every day since!"

Diner rubs the crease on her forehead, accidentally smearing her black-pepper gravy. "This is why I don't invite Tex over anymore."

"Why? Are you worried that he'd take your father's side?" Mom scowls.

"Maybe if your mother was more secure about her body, she wouldn't be so intimidated by Jel," Dad calls from the other room.

"As if she'd want an old-fashioned plate like you!" Mom snaps back.

"Neither of us are interested!" Dad calls. "You're literally the only one who's thinking about it, Talia." He turns the TV up, presumably to drown us out.

Mom grumbles and turns the page of the album. Most of the photos are of her and Dad right after they got married, when they presumably weren't fighting about some jiggly Jell-O secretary.

"Look how cute I was back then," Mom sighs. "Back when I was just a light bruschetta... Oh, and here's one where I'm a stuffed squash blossom! That's you, Diner."

"Wow," my sister drawls, "amazing. Having a baby definitely solved all your marital problems."

Mom's solution to dealing with things she can't control has been the same for my whole life: she ignores them. Instead of letting Diner's sarcasm get her down, she flips the page again. "Oh, look, I'm a stuffed tortellini here. You know what that means!"

Unfortunately, I do. The next page is full of pictures of baby-me. The earlier ones aren't too bad, when I'm just a single sugar pea or a fingerling potato. As the pictures jump through time, though, they start to mess with my head: I progress to a handful of goldfish crackers, then a side salad, then a garlic knot. I remember begging my mom to let me attend school as Cheerios, and the long conversation she had with me about how I was too old for that.

On the bright side, my parents accepted my gender identity early on. I was in third grade when I came out as transmasc, and they were totally supportive. Mom came with me to all my appointments, and even Dad never once got my pronouns wrong. I suppose I should be grateful, but as I sit there staring at my First Day of Sixth Grade photo, I gaze down at the personal pan pizza in that photo, with his greasy skin and unsmiling eyes, and I feel for him. I remember how poorly my old skin used to fit.

"Weren't you cute back then?" Mom asks.

Diner's lips press into a thin line. We've never been particularly close, but she went to bat for me when I came out to our parents in high school. "Mom," she says, in that warning tone.

Mom plows ahead. No matter how many times I ask her to drop it, she can't help herself. "All I'm saying is, you were such a *cute* dinner, Homestyle. I don't know why you insist on"—she waves her hand at me—"all this. I mean, it's family night. Can't you at least make an effort?"

"I *did* make an effort," I mumble.

Diner elbows her. "Knock it off, Mom."

It doesn't matter. Even if my mother didn't feel the need to bring this up every time I'm here, all of the family photos on the walls are from when I was still trying to play the part of a good little dinner. My dad hardly looks at me anymore. It's not the worst reaction they could have had, but it still hurts like hell.

Diner finally gets Mom to leave off with the photos and tells a long story about her most recent project at work, her wedding plans for next summer, and how her fiancé, Tex-Mex, is about to get a promotion.

Nobody asks about me. I appreciate the fact that Diner is pulling aggro again—she does that whenever there's an argument, because she's exactly what Mom and Dad want in a kid. She's successful, she's normal, and somehow, she's *happy*. Instead of feeling cramped and constrained by the life our parents pushed on her, she's perfectly at peace with herself.

There was a time when I wished that I felt the same, but if there's one thought that keeps me from spinning out over the course of the next few hours, it's the realization that I'm finally living the life I always craved but was told I couldn't have.

By the time I finally leave, I'm exhausted. I know Nat has to get up early for work tomorrow, but I need to hear her voice. I dial her number and put my phone on speaker before I even pull out of the driveway.

She sounds frazzled when she answers. "Hey, Homes. Everything okay?"

"Yeah. I'm just coming from a family dinner."

"Oh." There's understanding in her tone. "I seem to recall you saying that your family was kind of *meh*."

"They're fine," I say automatically. It's mostly true.

"Right. Should I be worried?"

"No, it's not a big deal. They're... they're not the worst."

"High praise," she says drolly. "Do you want to come over? I should clarify that I'll be getting ready for bed soon, since I have to be up at the ass-end of dawn, but I know how family can be."

I bite my bottom lip. "Are you sure?"

"I wouldn't offer if I didn't mean it."

"I'll see you soon, then." I hang up, and at the next red light, I put in her address and let the GPS guide me. It's started to drizzle, and rain streaks the windshield, so I have to go slower than usual. Time slows to a crawl.

I just want to be where she is.

By the time I reach Nat's apartment, the rain has picked up. I rush to the door of her building and duck inside, already shivering. I wish I'd thought to check the weather. It's really coming down, and I hate driving in thunderstorms. Even as I think it, a bolt of lightning cracks against the night sky, and an answering boom of thunder rolls through in its wake.

Nat greets me at the door. She's a bao bun today, the kind with no filling. Before I have a chance to say a word, she folds me in a steamy embrace.

"Hey," she says as she squeezes me. "Come on in."

I kick off my shoes by the doorway and follow her through to her room. We never made it in here the other night, and I ended up leaving so that she could go to bed on time.

Nat heads straight for the bed and pulls me in after, settling next to me and getting nice and cozy. I already feel better.

"Do you want to talk about it?" she asks.

I stare up at the ceiling and sigh. "Do I have to?"

"No. You don't have to do anything." Her breathing slows, and her eyes flutter shut. She must be exhausted.

"I can go, if you want," I whisper. "This is already helping."

Nat mutters something against my shoulder.

"What was that?"

"I missed you," she repeats.

Before long, she's snuffling in her sleep, but I lie awake to the distant boom of thunder and the drumming of rain on the windowpane. When I was a kid, thunderstorms used to terrify me.

Tonight, however, I feel safer than I have in a long time.

Chapter Nine

On Thursday morning, Homes is still snoring in my bed by the time I head to work. I'm grateful for the glut of quiche Lorraine orders this time, because I don't have to think. I spend the whole day in a daze.

Sleeping next to Homes was nice. I felt...

Well, I felt something that I'm not going to examine too closely. Not yet. I'm not ready to let my feelings get involved.

Other parts of me, however, are fully prepared to get more intimate. I woke up hot and bothered as a hearty helping of *gai pad pongali*. All day at work, I can't stop thinking about how it felt when he swallowed me the other night—I've never experienced anything that intense. Half the time, I can't even get myself off. I'll start thinking about work, or how long it's been since I've done the dishes, or what I'm going to do for lunches this week, and then it all falls apart. With Homes, I think things could be different.

I tell myself that it's just hormones, but then I imagine him pressed against me, his eyes fixed on mine as he blind-bakes my crust, and next thing I know, I have a soggy bottom. I'm already craving that intimacy, and I've connected with him in ways I've never connected with anyone else. It's like we're cooking from the same recipe.

By the time we're locking up, I've made up my mind. I text Homes, *You free tonight?*

I don't see his reply until I get home: *For you? Of course. Maybe an official date this time?*

God, this guy. I text back, *Absolutely. 7 o'clock.* I include an address.

Let's see if Homestyle can handle the heat.

"Wow, you really know how to charm a guy." Homes is already laughing as he strolls up. "Shopping? Really? You shouldn't have."

"I thought it might be fun." I scoop up a basket from the stack inside the door. "And trust me, this isn't a standard grocery. Miguel stocks the good stuff." I take Homes by the hand and lead him inside. He's an omelet today, no fixings.

"You look nice," he tells me, admiring the savory Thai loaf I changed into before leaving the house. He's watching me with that sweet shy smile of his. I'm absolutely going to corrupt this boy.

I can't wait.

"Thanks." I squeeze his hand. "You do, too."

He wrinkles his nose. "I'm so plain, though."

"Nothing wrong with plain," I tell him. "That's one of the reasons I brought you here."

Homes cocks his head. He still hasn't worked out where we are. He's so vanilla, and I adore him for it.

I wink at him and lead him deeper into the store. I watch Homes's face for the exact moment when he realizes where I've brought him.

"Oh my God." He crisps around the edges as he takes in a giant squirt bottle of sriracha. "Nat—"

"If you're uncomfortable, we can leave," I tell him. "I just thought we could experiment. If you want. I'm not sure what you're into, and maybe you're not either, but I figured it could at least get us talking about things."

He shuffles his feet, staring at the twist nozzle on the top of the bottle. I imagine him gently slipping it inside me, squeezing the container until hot sauce dripped down my thighs, then licking me clean again. Or maybe he'd want me to use it on him.

Maybe this was a bad idea. I've freaked him out. At the very least, I've gotten myself all worked up, and now I'm going to have to switch gears. There's still time to go for a walk in the park, maybe, or try to catch a movie...

My train of thought is interrupted when Homes squeezes my hand and pulls me deeper into the store. "Let's see what they have," he says.

We go down the first aisle. There's nobody there—this place is mostly empty on weeknights.

"Do you come here a lot?" There's a warbling note in Homes's voice.

"Sometimes. Mostly just for kewpie and ABC and things like that." When he squints at me, I explain, "Self-lubricants and marinades. Like I said, I've been single for approximately ever."

"I've never tried most of this stuff." Homes crouches down in front of one of the shelves. "I mean, I've watched videos on PorkHub, but I haven't really done much of anything myself."

"Is it because..." I fumble with the words.

"No real reason," he says. "I was happy keeping things simple. That's kind of my whole deal."

"But you're with me," I blurt. Oh, goodness. Is he with me? Are we exclusive? Do I want it to be?

Yes, I realize, I do.

Homes chuckles, unfazed by the fact that I'm suddenly the one freaking out. "You mean that things aren't simple with you?"

"Exactly."

"Why not?"

I blink rapidly, not sure how to answer. "Because that's what everyone else tells me?"

"I disagree." Homes pulls out a small jar, studying the label carefully, although I'm not convinced he's actually reading it. "I think it's pretty easy to be with you. Or, no, not easy. That makes it sound like you're not worth the effort. I guess what I mean is that I don't mind trying new things as long as they're with you. I trust you."

I suck in a breath. I don't know what to say to that. Why does he keep offering me compliments that don't feel right? I want to be trustworthy. I'm just not sure I am. What if I mess this up somehow?

What if I let him down?

Homes holds up the little jar. "Have you tried this?" he asks. "I'm going to have to rely on your expertise."

My eyes focus on the label, and I let out a snort of laughter. "Black bean and chili crunch? Yeah, it's good, but it's not for the faint of heart."

He grins as he gets to his feet, still holding the jar. "Sounds perfect."

My knees buckle, and I nearly topple over. So much for Homes being vanilla. He's more adventurous than I gave him credit for.

We wander the store, our conversation growing more casual as it progresses. The lighter the tone, the hotter I get. As we linger over honey mustard, *sambal oelek,* za'atar, and adobo, it occurs to me that I've never shopped for spices with anyone else. My exes either knew what they wanted or left it to me to spice things up in the bedroom. Homes is game to try new things, although I guess for him, *everything* is new. I've never cared about that sort of thing before, but I find myself coveting his firsts. After tonight, any time his tongue prickles with the numbing heat of Szechuan peppercorns, he'll think of me. The citrusy, hot-pepper brightness of chimichurri will forever be associated with me. Scotch bonnet salt and the thick chocolate savoriness of mole will always bring him back to me.

"Are you okay?" he asks, and I realize he asked me a question that I didn't hear.

"Yeah," I rasp. "Just thinking."

Homes leans in, whispering low and rough. "About me?"

All the damn time, I think. One taste of him, and I'm hooked.

But how long until he gets tired of me? What happens when I have nothing new to offer him?

I push my insecurities aside and steer him to the other side of the store. We've got a handful of seasonings to try out, and I want to see what else they've got.

The store mostly focuses on herbs and condiments, but there are a few basic cooking implements for sale as well: peelers, whisks, two varieties of garlic press.

"Kind of a disappointing selection," I observe.

Beside me, Homes makes a strangled sound.

I glance over at him, only to realize that he's staring at a small meat tenderizer as if transfixed. I reach for it. "Do you want to try this?"

"It's fine," he says hastily, trying to subtly rearrange the front of his cargo pants. His hand lingers a moment too long, cupping himself. "Oh my God, this is so embarrassing."

"It doesn't have to be." I set the basket down and pick up the meat tenderizer, slapping it twice in my palm. "That's why we're here, you know?"

"Nat." Homes averts his eyes. "*Please.*"

I'm not sure what he's begging for, so just to be safe, I set the meat tenderizer in the basket. "I'll pay for this stuff, if you want to head over to my place?" I can't imagine he'll want to wait in the checkout line, not with that grease stain spreading by his J-stitch.

"I'll meet you there?" he asks. When I nod, he bolts from the store. I stick around long enough to add an eggbeater to the basket before strolling up to the register.

Miguel grins as I hand over my goods. "Was that guy with you? He was in a big rush to get out of here."

"He's new," I explain. "To all of this."

"First time you've come in with someone in a while," Miguel observes as he rings me up. "Ever, maybe. Is this everything?"

I'm glad that he doesn't ask for an explanation. Before he

rings me up, I run back for a giant bottle of kewpie and a small shaker of za'atar.

"Just in case the night goes south?" Miguel asks.

"What are you talking about?" I wink. "These two go with everything."

Miguel's delighted laughter follows me out to my car.

Homes is already parked out front when I pull up to the curb outside my building. He's found a sweatshirt somewhere and tied it around his waist. I expected him to be sheepish, like he was in the shop, but the moment the elevator door closes behind us, he presses me to the wall, trapping my hands in a loose grip as he grinds against me, his kisses searing my mouth even before we reach my floor. I melt against him, almost dropping the bag of goodies I brought with me.

"Can you take the lead tonight?" Homes exhales against my neck, shivering at the idea of letting me be in charge, despite the fact that he's the one who pinned *me*.

"Yeah?" I nibble the edge of his omelet. "You want me to tenderize you, Homes?"

He shudders against me, only stumbling back when we reach my floor and the elevator dings.

We collapse into my apartment, a fumbling mess of desire. For once, I can't think of anything but the moment I'm inhabiting. No past. No future. No potential fallout. No consequences. Only this moment and the very next.

Mine, I think. *Mine, mine, mine.*

I shove him away from me, and for a moment, he looks hurt.

"Bedroom," I say. "Clothes off, now."

His eagerness returns. "Yes, ma'am," he says as I shepherd him down the hall to my room.

The moment we're inside, he shucks off everything he's wearing, revealing a sizable slice of thick-cut bacon. His Scotch eggs ride high and tight at the base of his pork belly.

I reach into the bag and produce the meat tenderizer, slapping it against my palm like I did in the store. Homes is mesmerized.

"You want me to use this on you?" I ask.

He nods, his mouth slightly open. A thick drop of bacon grease falls to the sheets between his thighs.

"I want to hear you say it." I take a step closer, wondering dimly how we got here. Since when am I someone who talks like this?

"Please, Nat." Homes's voice is steady this time, deeper than usual. He reaches between his legs to fondle his Scotch eggs, his eyes flicking from the mallet to my face and back again. "I want you to leave me tender. Please, baby, use me however you want."

I know there's an art to this, although it's been a long time since I used a tenderizer on anyone, and that wasn't exactly a thrilling experience for me. But now, with Homes staring up at me, exposed, I can see the appeal.

"The safeword," I tell him, "is banana yogurt."

And I reach down to take his throbbing bacon bits in my hand.

Chapter Ten

I've been known to get a little firm with my meat from time to time, but the way Nat handles me is like nothing else I've ever experienced. With each careful blow from the mallet, stars dance behind my eyes.

"Is that good for you, Homes?" she purrs, smacking me again, bringing me just to the edge of pain and no further.

All I can do is whimper her name. I'm hers. I would do anything she wanted right now. Anything.

And the fact that I get to experience all this with her makes me want to cry and scream and crumble into dust all at the same time.

I lie panting on the bed, my pork belly tenderer than it's ever been, breathless with wanting. I could finish from this, but I don't want to. I want her.

Just when I don't think I can take any more, Nat sets the mallet side. She reaches for the kewpie, which I didn't even see her pick up at the store. She straddles me, nestling my Scotch eggs between the folds of her loaf as she massages the slick mayo into my fatback.

"Nat," I pant, lifting myself up to kiss her. She slides open, cracking along the seams of her loaf.

"Not yet," she whispers into my mouth. "Not yet, Homes." The next thing I know, she's reaching for the eggbeater.

The thrum of it startles me, and Nat cries out, writhing against me. It occurs to me, in a distant and disinterested sort of way, that I could be self-conscious about this. That the fact that she needs implements might imply that I'm not enough.

To be honest, though, I've never felt more complete. More satisfied. It's enough that she wants me, that we get to be here together. I've got nothing to prove to anyone.

Once Nat is whipped to a frenzy, she tosses the beater aside and rolls to one side. "Get the sriracha," she gasps.

My hands shake as I remove the safety seal and untwist the nozzle. "Is this where you want it, baby?" I ask, kissing the widening seam between her halves.

"Uh huh." Her eyes are glazed, her loaf steaming, as I squirt a hot load of spicy ketchup into her.

"Oh, fuck." Nat's eyes roll back. "Homes, come here. I need you. Right now."

I set the bottle aside as she spreads for me, pulling open, blooming like a yeasty flower. I've never done this before, but she guides me, pulling me inside her, enveloping me fully. For a moment, I wonder if I've gotten it wrong, but then she closes around me, pressing me deep. I lose myself in her, and for a few blissful minutes that end much too soon, we stop being individuals and combine—in a frantic, thrusting slurry of kewpie and sriracha—into a singular egg-and-pork-belly *bánh mì*.

Afterward, we lie in a tangle of sheets and drippings, stuck together.

"Was that, um... good?" I ask.

"Good?" Nat laughs. "I wouldn't say that. That was the kind of meal that will change your life."

I kiss her forehead and smile up at the ceiling. "I'm still not sure this counts as a date."

Nat levers herself up on one elbow. "Are you complaining?"

I shake my head, gazing up at her. "No. No *way*. But I want it all, Nat."

"All?" she repeats, squirming until we're face to face.

"I want to spend time with you. I want to watch movies we both end up hating and complain about them over dessert. I want to play board games and pretend to let you win even though you really kicked my ass. I want to go on walks in the park or on the beach or whatever. I want to do all the goofy shit couples do."

She giggles. "You really are cheesy," she says. "But I like it. What do you want to do first?"

It's hard to think with her pressed against my side like that, still naked and slippery. "Um," I say, my more innocent fantasies of coupledom quickly swallowed by the rising tide of my hunger.

Nat grins. "*Um* sounds good," she says, pressing her lips to mine. "Maybe we can come back to all that other stuff later?"

I was a little worried that she'd want me to dine and dash, but not only does she insist that I stay for a few more courses, I end up sleeping in her bed, tangled up in her, as we slowly dissolve into one another.

Over the next few weeks, we spend more and more time together, although we have trouble keeping things sweet and clean. The next time I see her, we go grocery shopping together, making each other try on ridiculous outfits. Partway through, Nat calls me to the changing room to show me the stale Christmas sprinkles she's tried on, and I end up on my knees eating her out while she leans against the door and watches me with storm-dark eyes.

A few days later, I spend the night at her place, ostensibly with the intent of watching *Game of Scones*. We only manage to keep our hands off each other for three episodes before Nat presses me face down on the couch and licks all the chocolate frosting off of my Long John, then rides me until I inject her with a starburst of Bavarian cream.

Leftovers doesn't give me much grief for how little time I spend at the apartment. On the nights I do make it home, he listens to me wax poetic about Nat's many charms.

"You're smiling all the time, bud." He jostles my shoulder. "I've never seen you like this."

"I'm happy," I tell him, dreaming of a time when things become even more serious. "I feel like I have a future with her, you know?"

"Come here, you big sap." Leftovers wraps an arm around my burrito shell and digs his knuckles into my scrambled eggs and salsa verde. "When you're off making out with your girl, just don't forget your old pal Lefty."

Even family dinner nights aren't so bad. I don't mention Nat outright, but I think Diner can tell that something's up. Mom, of course, is still obsessed with Dad's maybe-not-an-affair with the jiggly Jell-O lady at work, but at least I know that I have people who like me for me, even if my family still brings up the meal I used to be from time to time.

Nat and I end up driving back to her place one night after work, and she returns me the next morning, walking me to the door of The Daily Grind before returning to the Pig-in-a-Poke. She's never invited me to her restaurant. She barely talks about it, despite all the time she spends there. I get it. I don't like to spend any more time than necessary thinking about work when I'm not there. That's probably the only reason she's never taken me by—right?

"You're here early," Jo observes as I walk in the door. I can tell by the cadence of her voice that she's only had one cup of coffee so far, two max. By midmorning, she'll be jittering all over the place.

I set my bag to one side and run my hand over my muffin top. "I got a ride to work with my *girlfriend*." Even now, the word is as sweet as powdered sugar on my tongue.

"Glad it's working out." Jo fires up the machine to pull another triple-shot espresso. "I need a little pick-me-up, and then I'm going to start on the baked oatmeal. You mind figuring out the cookie situation?"

I set to work right away, mixing and stirring while my mind wanders. This is the most I've ever imagined for myself, and I wonder if things will be just like this a year from now, and the next, and the next. Spending my days at a job I'm good at, and whiling away my nights and weekends with my dreamgirl. I've never had particularly lofty aspirations. This would be enough for me.

I wonder if Nat feels the same.

I'm still lost in a daydream when my phone goes off with a message. It's from Lefty: *Got plans Saturday. Won't be in all night. Don't do anything I wouldn't do, okay?* This is followed by every food emoji in the keyboard.

I check to make sure that Jo's occupied before firing off a quick text to Nat. *I've got the apartment to myself on Saturday. Want to come to my place for once?*

She must be busy opening her restaurant, but even so, her reply comes about three seconds later. *Hell yes.*

And for the whole rest of the day, I can't stop smiling.

Chapter Eleven

Homes's place is a little smaller than mine, and somewhat shabbier. I'm a bit of a cluttercore decorator, but at least there's a system.

As I step through the door, he bends in for a kiss. "Did you find the place okay? Was there enough parking?"

I slide my long jacket off my shoulders as I step past him. "Yup, it all went smoothly."

Homes closes the door behind me. "You can hang your coat here—" he begins, but when he turns and sees me, he chokes.

I'm nothing but plain pancakes underneath.

Homes's mouth hangs open as I sashay past him, giving him an eyeful of my golden-brown tone. I take my time hanging my jacket on the peg, then bend down to slip off my shoes, wiggling my fluffy batter as I do so.

"Holy shit, Nat," Homes squeaks.

I look over my shoulder at him. I've never been this bold before in my life, but then again, I've never met anyone else who makes me feel so desirable. Homes is staring at me like I'm a full buffet and he can't wait to dig in.

"You like what you see?" I ask.

"Yes," he croaks without a moment's hesitation. "God, yes. Tell me what you want, Nat."

"I. Want. You." I wait until his eyes meet mine before taking a step closer. "I want it all. I want you to smother me in your fruits." My words come out breathless and rough, but I can't stop. "I want your toppings, Homestyle. *All of them.*"

Homes groans and lunges toward me. Before I have time to think, he's pressed against me, covering me like a butter pat and melting into every inch of exposed flapjack. I've never been so in tune with another person, and yet so wholly myself. In seconds, his caress leaves me slick and oiled and succulent.

"Nat," he groans. "Oh, *God,* you're so absorbent tonight."

"Only for you," I breathe. He pulls away, and I can already feel myself cooling to room temperature. "No, don't stop..."

He pulls me upright and leads me toward his room. I trip over myself in my eagerness to feel him melt into me again. So much for being the one in control of the situation. Every other time we've been together, I've been the one in charge. No complaints there, but tonight, I want things to be different.

Homes takes his time closing the door behind me and drawing me down to the bed. This time, I'm the one trembling as he explores every fold of my short stack, leaving each layer a buttery mess in his wake.

I pant his name. "Stop playing with me, Homes. I want you to top me."

I can hear the laughter in his voice as he whispers in my ear. "Naughty girl. I want to hear you beg first." He licks me right in my buttered middle, and the room spins. Turnabout is fair play. I'm drunk on him. I've been drunk on him for weeks. On the few nights we've spent apart, I've been riding the eggbeater, desperate for release that never comes. The vibrating silicone sausage that's been my constant companion for years isn't enough. No matter how much mayo I spread on it, no matter how high I turn the settings, it doesn't compare to his breath in my ear or the savory sounds he makes when it's *his* kielbasa inside me.

"Please, Homes." I'm already beyond shame, dripping with refined fats and hot off the griddle. "*Please.*"

"Good girl," he whispers, and he covers my top layer in a cinnamon apple compote. He's aromatically spiced but not too sweet, with more cardamom and nutmeg than sugar, and his apples are still firm and toothsome. He's juicy enough that his drippings seep into me without leaving me inedible.

"Yes," I breathe. "Oh, Homes, that's so *good.*"

"I want to try something," he says. "How do you feel about, um..." He heats up a little and starts to scrape himself away. "Never mind."

"Homes. Tell me."

He takes a deep breath before whispering, "Playing with some maple syrup."

I'm sticky now, but still holding my shape. It's my turn to reheat. "Do you really think I would have come over in this state if I *didn't* like the idea?" I ask breathlessly.

He trembles against me. "Are you sure?"

"If it's with you, I'm sure," I tell him. "I even thought about coming over as Dutch cream waffles and letting you fill each individual cavity right to the brim, but... Well, I've never done this before, so..."

"Nor have I." Homes nibbles at my edges. "Obviously. And I never thought I'd be into it, but being with you makes me want things that I never even considered before. Are you sure about this?"

"I'm sure." One glance from Homes turns me into a cinnamon red hot. "Just take it slow. And let's not try any flavors this time, if that's okay?"

"For you, Nat, I'll be pure maple syrup. No corn syrups or substitutes." He hoists himself back onto his knees and positions his drip dispenser.

I brace myself for the first drops. What would Keto think if she could see me now? What would my parents think? They're such traditional breakfast items. And Keto would be horrified by all the natural sugars involved.

Then the first viscous amber drop hits me, and I no longer care what people think. This feels so *right*.

"Are you okay, Nat?" Homes asks in a nervous voice.

"More," I gasp, unable to think straight. As the syrup soaks into my already buttered dough, I shudder with satisfaction. His syrup is sweet and dark, without the faintest hint of anything artificial, undercut with a deep caramel bouquet. I'm saturated with him, but I don't tell him to stop. I want him to drizzle me until I become a soggy mess, until I'm more syrup than pancake.

"Nat," Homes croaks. "I don't think I can hold back anymore."

"Nobody asked you to." I draw him deeper into my batter. "I told you. I want you. All of you."

In one smooth motion, he flips me over. I gasp as he fumbles with his sausage, buttering my folds with his free hand. Then his turgid pig slides into my willing blanket, right where he belongs.

"I'm not going to last," he warns me, but I'm already falling apart around him. Every inch of me is impregnated with his golden shower, and I'm sodden from his earlier fruit topping. I lose track of myself, and before I know it, Homes is gasping above me. At the last minute, he pulls away, covering the exposed bottom of my short stack in spritz after spritz of aerosolized whipped cream. There's no time to whip his own, but I'm beyond caring. He doesn't stop until his can runs out with a final, dry hiss.

"God, Nat," he pants, "do you have any idea what you do to me?"

I can't move. I can't speak. All I can do is float in a sugar-sweet haze of post-coital bliss.

I've been more *complicated* meals, but I've never been so damn satisfied.

I don't know how much time passes before Homes finally slips out of bed. When he returns, he starts wiping up the melting mess of whipped cream and syrup.

"I may have gone overboard," he says sheepishly.

"No," I mumble. "It was perfect. *You* were perfect."

He presses his forehead to my back. "Stop," he mumbles.

"I'm serious." I roll over to face him. "It's never been like that with anyone else. I'm usually a savory condiment type of girl. But you make me want to indulge."

He stares down at me from his spot on the edge of the bed. There's hope in his face, and longing—not hunger, like when he looked at me earlier, but hope. "Nat," he begins.

I can see what he's going to say before the words leave his lips: *I love you.* My first instinct, my *only* instinct, is to panic. I like Homes, of course I do. Judging by what we just did, what we've been doing for weeks in all sorts of configurations and locales, I *more* than like him. But love's a big word, and it feels like a promise that I'm not ready to make.

I rocket to my feet. "I need a shower," I blurt.

He nods. "Of course. Shower's all yours." He waves one hand toward the bathroom, and I bolt for safety.

What are you doing? I ask myself as I start the water. *What's the big deal if he says three words to you? It's not like you're obligated to say them back. You can thank him and explain that you're not there yet. It wouldn't be the end of the world. He'd forgive you.*

The thought of watching the excitement slowly fade from his face, however, is enough to crush me flatter than a silver dollar pancake. I don't date. We're not even official, technically. I'm not ready for this. I wasn't looking for love, and now that my brain isn't fogged with hormones, I'm not sure what I want with Homes.

This part is fun. It feels good.

But I'm not ready to turn this fling into a full-fledged commitment. Not with the L-word involved.

I step into the shower just long enough to avoid having to explain myself, then slip back into the bedroom wrapped in a towel. "I'm just gonna grab my things," I blurt, before remembering that I came over in nothing but a trench coat. "I've got to be up early tomorrow, so I'll head out now. Thanks for a good time."

I bolt for the living room before Homes has a chance to utter a single word.

Chapter Twelve

Leftovers strolls into the apartment on Sunday morning, takes one look at my face, and asks, "Christ on a crêpe, dude, did she dump you?"

"No," I mutter. I've been sitting on the couch since last night, rolled up in an afghan and staring dead-eyed at the TV.

"Okay, man. Talk to me." Leftovers flops down beside me. His gaze is like a weight on my shoulders, and I avoid his eyes until I start to squirm under his attention. When I glance over at him at last, words fail me.

"Lefty?" I gasp.

"In the flesh, bro."

I point at his chest. "Explain yourself."

"What?" He shrugs sheepishly. "Just a little something I cooked up earlier. *Nāc rītā atkal* isn't that fancy."

I don't know what the hell he just said, but the fact remains that my usually sloppy roommate looks handsome as fuck today. It makes me feel even worse about how things went with Nat last night, which I didn't think was possible.

"Is that even a leftover?" I size him up. "Looks like a meat crêpe."

"Get on my level, young man," Leftovers says, with all the

gravitas of a college professor. "*Nāc rītā atkal* literally means 'come back tomorrow.' It's *always* leftovers."

"Sorry I'm not up to date on my Czechoslovakian," I mutter.

"A, it's Latvian, and B, stop trying to change the subject. Who put bastard powder in your cornflakes this morning? I'm trying to ask what's up with you, because unlike my *delectable* self, you look like something that was left out of the fridge overnight."

It's true. I'm nothing but a soggy fruit cup today. Thank God I don't have to go to work, because Jo would sense a problem a mile away, and I don't have it in me to explain myself today.

"Nat came over last night," I explain.

"And you fucked like rabbits, I assume."

I cough. "I never said that."

"The whole house smells like melted butter and maple syrup, little buddy. You don't *have* to say anything. So stop beating around the brioche. You rode the train to pound town, and then what?"

"Nothing. She left." I rub my palms against my eyes.

"Okay..." Leftovers lets the unfinished thought linger in the air between us.

"I may have... I... I may have tried to tell her—"

Leftovers recoils in horror. "*Please* tell me that you didn't blurt out anything weird while you were sucking her beef curtains."

I gag. "That's foul, Lefty. Don't talk about her like that. Don't talk about *me* like that."

"Fine." Lefty grins. "So you were nutting her fruitcake, and—"

"Please stop." I smack him.

"Hey, at least you're smiling right now." He's far too pleased with himself, all things considered. "Spill the beans, Homesie. What's the problem?"

"Okay, okay, geeze. Everything we did was *great*. And then I tried to tell her I loved her, and she freaked out and left."

Leftovers's eye twitches. "You *what*?"

"You heard me."

"Okay." He bends forward, resting his elbows on his knees. "Okay."

A spark of annoyance flares in my chest. "Can we please *not* do the toxic macho thing where we act like discussing our feelings is a bad thing? I like Nat. I *more than* like Nat. If your advice is going to be something along the lines of, '*Never say I love you first,*' then I don't need it."

Leftovers sighs. "Have a little faith, huh, Homesie? I'm not going to say that. I mean, was your timing kinda shit? Yes. Is blurting out big feelings in the throes of post-coital bliss the *best* way to tell a lady-type you love her? No. But I didn't realize you were that serious about her."

I clench my jaw. "Well, I *am*."

"Okay. That's cool." He nudges me gently. "But if I'm surprised, then it stands to reason that she might be surprised, too. Have the two of you ever talked about intention? Like, what you're dating *for*? Is she looking for love or is she looking for a fling?"

My stomach dips down, the juices pooling beneath my over-ripe melon chunks. "Oh." All my daydreams burst like bubbles blown through a straw into chocolate milk. "Oh, no."

Leftovers nods sympathetically. "Never talked about it, huh?"

"No, but I think... I think maybe the latter." I'm an idiot. I told Jo she was my girlfriend. I remember telling Nat that I wanted to do couples stuff, but did we ever agree to be official? Or did I just assume? She talked about not wanting to date, but...

But I thought I was different. That I was special.

I bury my face in my hands to hide.

"Well, that sucks." Leftovers leans back and studies me. "Have you texted her, or vice versa?"

I shake my head miserably.

"I think you should. Tell her how you feel."

"I'm sorry, what?" I wrinkle my nose, lifting my head again. "Isn't that what started this whole mess?"

"For one thing, there's a difference between texting and shouting '*I love you*' while you're egging all over her face."

"*Lefty, I swear—*"

"For another, if she felt the same way, she probably wouldn't have freaked out. But maybe she would. Maybe she was in a relationship that made her gun-shy. Maybe she's not interested in anything long term. Maybe there's something else going on, and all I'm saying is, you won't *know* until you talk to her. So talk to her! Communication is hot, dude. Chicks love that shit."

I stare at him for a long moment. Leftovers has been my best friend for a long time, and he's a good guy, but I'm starting to wonder if I underestimated him. Between that devil-may-care surface, I think he might actually be some sort of well-baked love guru.

"I'll reach out," I say. "And by the way, where were *you* last night?"

"What?" Leftovers shrugs. "Nothing. Nowhere. Out."

"Practicing your communication?" I ask, my tone as dry as a stale toaster pastry.

"Maybe." He gets up off the couch.

"Are you sure that you don't want to help me write this text?"

"Nah, Homes. You've got this by now. I believe in you." He smacks my arm a couple of times for good measure. "I've taught you everything I know, young papadam. Now it's your time to shine."

I pull out my phone and start drafting a text.

Chapter Thirteen

I wake, groggy and irritable, to the sound of my phone ringing.

"Don't want this," I say aloud to no one. "Don't want phone calls on Sunday. It's bad news. It's gonna be *her*."

The phone goes silent for a moment, then buzzes again.

Dammit. Now I know for sure who it is.

I roll over in bed and grope blindly for my cell. I realize a moment too late that I'm not getting a phone call. I'm on the receiving end of a FoodTime.

And, sure enough, it's my mother.

I sit up in bed and try not to look like death warmed over, pasting a smile on my face seconds before I answer.

"Hello, Mae!" I grin at the screen with an enthusiasm I don't feel. I wish I hadn't left Homes last night. I wish I hadn't panicked. He's so sweet. I'm sure that we could have talked things out, given the chance. I could have said something nice and mature like, *Hey, I totally believe your feelings, and I want to acknowledge them while also making it clear that I don't feel the same way right now.* You know, like a fucking adult. Instead, I fled for the hills and spent half the night tossing and turning, riddled with regret and griddled with guilt.

"Ooh, International Fusion, you look so very bad today." My mother clicks her tongue. She, of course, is a pristine serving of *khao neow moo ping*, with her sticky rice wrapped in a perfectly-folded banana leaf and two pork skewers resting on top. When I was little, I used to hope that I could grow up to look like my mom.

I'm still hoping, but so far, no dice. My video shows that I'm literally just half a dragonfruit today.

Yikes.

"I didn't sleep so well, Mae," I tell her.

"No, I can see this. And it is so late! Usually you are an early bird getting the gummy worm. Is everything all right, my daughter?"

Sometimes I wish that my mother was the sort of person that I could go to for advice. Sometimes I wish so hard that I convince myself she is.

Not that it's ever worked before, but there's a first time for everything.

"I'm sort of, um..." I pull my knees up to my chest. "Sort of seeing someone?"

My mother's eyes widen farther than I thought was possible. *"Khon dii! Come here! Your daughter has found a boyfriend!"*

Bold of her to assume that I'm dating a guy—not that I ever gave much thought to gender or meal identity before I met Homes. She has no reason to assume otherwise, though, so I tell myself that her knee-jerk assumptions aren't an omen of any kind. Is my mom a TERB?

This is not how I wanted to start my day.

My father, a resplendent *açaí na tigela*, comes puffing in from the next room. "Did I hear rightly, *amorzinho*? Is my little girl in love?"

"Nobody said that I was in love, Papai." I bury my face in the sheets. Kill me now. "I'm seeing someone. *Casually*."

"I am already planning the wedding," my mother announces. "I have been thinking on this every day since you were a little girl. It will be so lovely—"

"Mom. Chill." Maybe I should hit Brunch up after this. I could use a drink. "Nobody's talking about marriage."

"I am," my mother announces.

"Tell us everything." My father is doing a little dance in the background. They're too much. When they aren't annoying the hell out of me or getting on my case about my potential and how I may or may not be living up to it, I adore them.

But I also don't know what to tell them.

"What do you want to know?" I ask warily.

My mother counts her answers off on her fingers. "Well, let me see. What is his name? Where is he from? What does he do? How many siblings does he have?"

My father butts in. "Does his father have all of his pork floss? They say that this is a very good indication of how he will look when he's older." He preens for the camera, showing off his full head of hair. It's very impressive, I'm sure.

It's also very much beside the point.

"His name is Homestyle," I begin. "He's from around here. He works in the food industry." No need to mention that he's a part-time barista, they'll just make a whole thing about it, and it's none of their business. "As far as his family, I can't tell you much. I haven't met them, because again, *casual.*" Although from what Homes has told me, they're not great.

"Yes, yes, we are all very impressed with your lack of commitment." My mother flaps a hand at the screen. "What else can you tell us? What else is important?"

"Um..." I consider what else to tell them. Realistically, even if we dated, Homes's past would be none of their business. I know the gender stuff wouldn't matter to them, my parents aren't *fossils,* but what about the rest? I don't think that they'd be weird about it even if I *did* tell them.

But what if they were? What if they were horrified to learn that Homes's parents are dinners?

And what if that reflected poorly on me?

"Um, nope." I scratch the back of my neck. "Nothing much."

"Maybe we can meet this boyfriend of yours next time you visit?" my mother suggests. "Or we can come to visit you?"

I let out an involuntary squeak. "He's not my boyfriend! Because, as I have said several times already, we're—"

"Casual," all three of us say in unison, with varying degrees of nonplussed-ness.

"I hear what you are saying." My mother shakes her head. "But I have never known you to do things by halves, my daughter. If you like this Homestyle enough to tell us, then he must be very special to you."

"Yeah." I feel like I'm something that got stuck to the bottom of a boot. Homes is special to me, so why do I feel this way? Why am I so reluctant to share details with my parents, or to have the conversations with him that terrify me?

Between my relationship and my restaurant, I feel like I've been doing everything by halves lately.

"I need to get dressed. Did you need something, or...?"

"Just checking in." My mother smiles at me. "And it is a good thing, too, or you might never have told us you were getting married."

"I'm not—!" I begin.

"She never tells us anything!" My father swoons dramatically in the background.

"She needs her space," my mother says. My parents not only love the Good Cop, Bad Cop routine, they like to switch things up just to keep it fresh.

"Goodbye, Mae! Goodbye, Papai!" I wave to the screen before ending the call. I can finally stop smiling. What a relief.

I lie in my bed, staring up at the ceiling, wondering what I've gotten myself into. I feel like I'm teetering on a ledge, and I need someone to talk me down.

Well, that's feasible, at least. I pick up my phone again, preparing to text Keto, when I see that I missed a message from Homes during my FoodTime chat.

Two lines in, and I can tell that I'm going to need food before I deal with this one.

. . .

"Hi, Nat. I just wanted to say that last night was amazing... blah blah, intimate details that I'm not sharing... Okay, here we go. *I'm sorry if I made you uncomfortable. Judging by the way you fled the room, I'm guessing I did. I want you to know that I care about you. Deeply. Not just when we're being physical, either. I love you all the time. I don't need you to say it, but I need you to hear it. And if that's a problem, I'd like to know now, before I say anything else that will hurt one or both of us."* I lift my eyes to Keto's face.

Her mouth hangs open as she absorbs what I've just read aloud. "The fuck?"

"The fuck indeed," I agree.

Keto looks around the juice bar. She's short staffed today, so my options were to wait until after closing time, or talk to her at work on one of her breaks. All things considered, waiting wasn't an option, and as far as I know, Homes has never come to the juice bar. This should be private enough for our purposes. Her business slows down this late in the day, so my friend has joined me at a table with two Green Goddess juices, which also happens to be what she is today.

"Okay, first of all." Keto holds up a finger. "Ew."

I lower my phone. "Ew?" That's not how I'd put it. My thoughts on reading, in chronological order, were: *cute, how is he so honest,* and *help.*

"Yeah, I mean, read the room." She gestures to indicate her half-empty establishment. "You two are banging, but you're not, like, an item. Yikes, right? Or maybe one big yike."

"I'm... sorry?"

"Oh, come on." Keto rolls her eyes as she slurps her verdant drink. "Look, I know we feel differently about the used-to-be-a-dinner thing, and that's cool of you. I mean, it would bother *me,* but whatever. But you're way out of his league. He's a part-timer at a coffee place, for goodness' sake. Sure, he's a snack, but he's like..." Keto scoffs. "He's a cheat food."

I stare at her, unable to form words.

"Oh, come on. I'm right, and you know it. He'll be fun for a while, but it's not going to last. Onward and upward. I figured you'd keep him around until something better came along, but if he's gonna get all clingy like that, cut him loose before he starts getting ideas. It'll just get ugly otherwise."

Keto's tone suggests that she thinks she's in the right here, but I can't believe what I'm hearing. I know that she doesn't care much for Homestyle, but I thought we'd gotten past the TERB crap by now. I didn't realize that she'd written off Homes entirely.

It's like I haven't been seeing her clearly this whole time, and all of a sudden, she's come into focus. This is what Keto's like. She sees people as disposable, and she thinks I do, too.

"Why would I dump him?" I ask slowly. I want to hear her say it.

Keto scoffs. "Why? Come on, the real question is, why *wouldn't* you? It's not like you two have a future together." She reaches across the table to pat my hand, which sits stiff and wooden between us. "What does a guy like that have to offer someone like you? I mean, no offense." She lowers her voice. "But you're running a great restaurant, and you're finally fitting in here... No, don't make that face, you know it's true. You were kinda, I dunno, weird before." She shrugs and pulls a face that implies that she feels guilty about what she's telling me. And yet here she is, saying it.

Again.

Keto squeezes my hand. "Do you really want to be seen with someone like, you know. Like *him?*" She lifts her eyebrows meaningfully.

In that moment, I realize what she's getting at, and my mouth snaps shut. She has a point. When Homes tried to confess to me, and again when I was on the phone with my parents, I held back because I was afraid of what other people would think about me if they connected the two of us. I try to imagine introducing Homes to my parents, not knowing how they'll react to him, and a molasses pit of guilt opens in my belly.

What would being with Homes say about me? Would it change how people think about me? I'm not even brave enough to celebrate the parts of myself that other people judge.

I hear myself saying, "I don't know." Because I don't. Until this exact moment, I didn't realize how hard I was trying to mask my true self in front of other people, including my friends and family. I didn't realize how much I valued having control over what I showed them.

A shadow falls over the table, and both of us look up. I don't immediately recognize the guy standing over us and glaring down at Keto, holding a bundle of roses. *She* does, however, and her bright green face somehow manages an even more acidic tint.

"Oh, hey, Lefty." She smiles, but it strikes me as fake, even more put-on than the plastic grin I wore for my parents this morning. Her eyes drift toward me. "Fancy seeing you here. What brings you by?"

Leftovers drops something on the table with a clatter. His eyes never leave Keto's face. "I accidentally grabbed your keys on the way out the door this morning. Thought you might need them."

"My keys?" Keto grimaces. "How did you... um..."

I suck in a breath. "Whoa, hold up. Are you two—?" I point at each of them with an index finger, then bump them together side-by-side.

"No," Keto blurts, at the same time that Leftovers coldly utters, "Yes."

Keto lets out a little whine of dismay as Lefty turns his frosty gaze on me. "I'm her *cheat food*," he snarls. At first, I think that he's only mad at her, but his eyes narrow even further when they meet mine. "Just like Homesie is yours."

"I didn't say that." My words come out sharp and prickly.

"True," he snaps. "But he deserves someone better than a lover who runs out when he tries to talk to her and badmouths him behind his back."

"I didn't—" I start to say, but Leftovers turns away from me. He doesn't want to hear it from me.

And really, is he wrong?

"I thought we agreed to keep things on the DL," Keto wheedles.

"Is that what you thought? Or did you just not want your friends to know we were smashing so that when something else better came along, you could easily cut me loose?"

Keto bites her lip, which is all the answer Leftovers needs. Still clutching the bouquet, he turns on his heel and stomps toward the front door. People are staring now: the gluten-free chicken Caesar wrap behind the counter, the cottage cheese fruit parfait couple by the door, the cluster of sausage-and-egg sandwiches waiting in line to order, even the breakfast pizza typing on his laptop in the back corner.

"Lefty, wait!" Keto calls just as his palm hits the push bar.

"For what?" His laugh is bitter and he turns to face her. "For you? After what I opened up to you about last night, you really think I want to waste my time with someone who talks about my best friend like that? Who acts like they don't know me? Hell no, dude." He cuts his eyes toward me. "Nice job not rocking the boat, Nat. Great friend you got here." He pushes his way through the door. The sky is overcast, and just as the door slams behind him, the first drizzle of rain hits the plate glass windows.

With a snarl that's audible from inside, Leftovers slams the bouquet of roses into the trash, shoots Keto one last disgusted glance, and storms off.

I'm in shock, not just because of this revelation about my friend, and not just because I'm ashamed that Leftovers overheard my undeniable silence.

He stood up to Keto, and he left.

It's something I'm not sure I would ever have had the guts to do.

I shoot to my feet and toss the last of my juice in the trash on my way to the door. Keto doesn't even try to stop me. She's still staring after Leftovers with a heartbroken expression that's so utterly unlike her, I can scarcely believe it.

For once, I don't care to know what she thinks. I just want to get away from her.

Too bad I can't get away from myself in the process.

Chapter Fourteen

I'm napping on the couch to the soothing sounds of Guy Hungry telling off an unlucky contestant when the door opens again.

"Nat?" I ask, before I really register what's going on.

It's Leftovers. He's soaking wet, and his crêpe skin is flaking off of him in leaves. He totters through the doorway, kicks off his shoes, and collapses onto the couch, a sodden mess. Every ounce of confidence is drained from his posture and his face.

"Hey, hey, hey." I turn off the TV and wrap one arm around his shoulders. "What's wrong? Talk to me, Lefty."

He lets out a hiccup, which is my first indication that at least some of the moisture on his face is the result of tears and not just the rain that's currently battering against the windowpane.

"I've been sleeping with Keto," he blurts.

"Um." I rub circles on his back. "...good for you?"

"And she's the fucking worst." He looks up at me with wide, stricken eyes. "I swung by her shop to drop off her keys and take her some flowers. I'd never been there before, and I thought it might be cool to see her place, I guess?"

"It *wasn't* cool, I take it?"

"No." He scrubs at his eyes. "No, it wasn't cool at all. She was talking to your girl and saying all kinds of shit, and when I tried to call her out on it, she lied about sleeping with me."

"Wait." I freeze. "Nat was there?" He's throwing a lot at me, and to be honest, I'm having trouble keeping up.

"Yeah, dude." Leftovers shudders. "I don't know what you texted her, but she's not the one."

"Hang on." I push myself into a ball against the arm of the couch. "I don't understand."

"It's pretty simple. Keto's a user, and Nat's no better. If you could have heard the things that came out of that girl's mouth—"

"Keto's mouth, right?" I clarify.

Leftover shakes his head. "Keto said a lot of shit, my dude, and Nat was nodding along."

I shift away from him, closer to the arm of the couch. "Nat isn't like that."

Lefty's eyes are full of pity. "Isn't she?"

I hesitate, thinking back to that time in the coffee shop when Keto bad-mouthed me within a few dozen feet of the register, and how Nat just... sat there. Listening, but not talking.

I open my mouth, prepared to offer some sort of alternate explanation. Maybe it was a misunderstanding. Maybe Leftovers misconstrued something.

But I've known Lefty for a long time. Longer than almost anyone. When I came out to him, he didn't say, *Maybe you've misunderstood who you are.* He was there for me, more than anyone else was. More than anyone ever has been to date.

So I do him the same courtesy. I believe him, even though it's like taking a knife to the crust.

"Oh, Lefty." I wrap my arms around him and squeeze him tight.

He starts to say something, but pounding on the front door makes both of us sit up straight. Leftovers stares at the door with such intensity that I half expect him to burn holes in the wood with his eyeballs.

The knock comes again, a little musical rhythm, and a soft voice calls, "Homes? Are you there?"

"Nat?" I don't even think before I respond.

Leftovers makes a little growl of frustration in the back of his throat. Come to think of it, he's always been my guard dog. Knowing him, he's more upset by the way Nat acted than by the way Keto did. The guy's burned a lot of bridges on my behalf.

"I'm going to get that," I say, but I don't rise to my feet until Leftovers nods.

I totter to the door and take a deep breath before turning the knob.

Nat is standing in the hall, her dark eyes slick with tears, her seed-studded fruit dropping with rainwater. My first instinct is to throw my arms around her and pull her into the house, towel her off, and get her a mug of mint tea.

But instead, every muscle in my body locks up, and I do nothing at all.

Nat shuffles awkwardly from foot to foot. "Can I come in?" she asks.

I look to Leftovers for confirmation, and he grunts his assent. "Let her in. We don't want another noise complaint."

I step out of the way, and Nat shuffles past me, dripping onto the carpet. She casts Leftovers a pitying smile. "I'm really sorry about what Keto said."

"Yeah," he growls. "I bet you are."

"Homes." She turns to face me, the picture of contrition. I can't believe that she was here last night, that we... did what we did. I want desperately for her to say something, to explain herself in a way that makes sense.

I want to be wrong about her, but judging by her obvious penitence, I'm doubtful that a satisfactory explanation will be forthcoming. I don't think I'm going to like whatever she has to say.

"Here's the thing." She picks at her bright pink peel, so brilliant against the black-flecked flesh of her fruitmeats. "Keto can be, um... kind of awful."

"I know," I say. *I've heard.*

"So I wanted to come over and explain. The thing is, she gets a lot of stuff wrong."

"And you don't correct her," Leftovers snaps.

Nat takes a deep breath. "No, I don't. Because I'm still figuring things out. Keto's friendship is really important to me."

"Why?" Lefty stumbles to his feet. "Why are you so desperate to please her?"

Nat reaches for my hand. "Can we have this conversation in private?"

I pull back, crossing my arms over my chest. "I'd actually like an answer to that question, too."

Nat squeezes her eyes shut and withdraws, both physically and mentally. I watch her close up right before my eyes. "Keto makes me feel normal," she says.

I bite the inside of my cheek. It's tempting to speak up, to comfort her, to feed the words I want to hear into her mouth, but I don't. I can't. My jaw is wired shut, and I am as silent as a refrigerator during a power outage.

"You don't understand," she says. Her words come out in a rush, tumbling over each other, so fast that it's hard to follow. "I've always been weird. I've always stood out. People can take one look at me and just *know* that I'm different. I never had friends before I moved here, not like you have with Leftovers." She nods to my roommate, whose soggy mess of a body is dripping in globs onto the carpet. "I don't belong in the places my family is from, I didn't belong in the place where I grew up, and even after I moved here, I had to choose between being myself and being accepted. I just want to *fit* somewhere, Homes." She lets out a little sob.

"You fit with me," I tell her, already dreading her rejection.

Nat swallows hard, crossing her arms over her fruity bits in a mirror of my own closed posture. "I'm tired of being weird," she says. Her words are spoken soft as spun sugar, but they slice me open like really pointy corn chips on a tender palate.

"And I'm weird," I finish for her, saying aloud what she's only brave enough to imply.

Nat looks away, nodding her head once.

It's not a surprise, exactly. People have always looked at me funny. At school, other kids knew that there was something strange about me even before I did. I've never been good at keeping my head down and blending in, and even when I do—even when I manage to mask or pass or fall in with the right crowd—I can never let my guard down, because I know what can happen if I do. How cruel people can be. How they can hurt you even when they're trying not to.

I wish I could take Nat in my arms and tell her that it will be okay, that she deserves the world. I want to console her.

But I'm also smart enough to read between the lines, and I know where this is going.

"You feel like you have to choose between being yourself and fitting in. I get that, Nat, trust me. More than you know. But it sounds like you might need to decide which one matters to you more." My fever spikes. My stomach roils like I've come down with a particularly bad case of food poisoning, but I force myself to keep talking. "I don't want to be a cheat food, or a dirty secret. I told you how I feel. I love you. How do you feel about me?"

Her eyes search my face, and as the silence stretches on, I realize that she's already answered.

She likes me, *but*.

She's happy to come over for a dine and dash, *but*.

She wants to be with me, *but*.

I turn my back on her. "I think you should go."

I wish that she'd reach for me, that she'd tell me I've got it all wrong, that she'd rather be her real self with me than keep living a lie every time she talks to her backstabbing, toxic best friend.

Instead, the front door creaks, and when I glance over my shoulder as I step into my bedroom, Leftovers is standing alone in the living room, and Nat is gone.

I collapse onto my bed where the buttery, baking-soda scent

of her lingers. Last night, she was here with me, and she'll never be here again.

"Homes?" Leftover's voice wafts in from outside my door, and he taps the wood twice.

I don't know if he's checking in on me, or if he wants to talk to someone about his breakup with Keto. I know he's hurting, too, and I wish I could fix it. I wish I could make things easier for Nat, and that I could make Keto apologize for the shitty way she's treated my friend and my ex.

My ex.

Nat is my ex.

For all my wishing, the only thing that I have the strength to do is curl up around my pillow and bury my face in it so that it will absorb the flood of my tears.

Nat was supposed to be my dreamgirl.

After tonight, though, I never want to see her again.

Chapter Fifteen

Monday morning finds me in a fugue state as I go through the motions at the Pig-in-a-Poke. I don't have the energy to be angry that nobody orders the special. I have nothing left. I'm caught between righteous indignation—why should I pay for what Keto said?—and bone-deep disappointment in myself.

If I don't speak up for myself, why should I be expected to speak up for anybody else? There's a logic to the thought process, but it's flimsy at best.

Despite my inner turmoil, I somehow manage to be moderately put-together. I'm manioc with bananas and nut butter, a favorite of my father's. I guess I'm looking for a little comfort food today.

We're busy enough, and India knows my resting bitch face well enough, that nobody bothers me until we're closing up for the day. It's not until I exit the kitchen that my employees descend on me to give me the third degree.

"How are things going with your *boyfriend?*" India sing-songs.

I lean against the counter and close my eyes. "Can we not talk about this?"

"Did he break your heart?" Monty smacks his fist against his palm. "Ooh, I'll give him the old what for, just you tell me where to find him."

"I'm not talking about this," I protest. "It would be wildly unprofessional. I'm your boss."

"And our friend." India crosses her arms. "Come on, Nat, tell us what happened. We'll support you."

"I—" My head is killing me, this conversation is ridiculous, and I know that I'm not in the right. I *know* it. But I've felt like crap ever since I got Homes's text last night, and I need to tell *someone.* Before I can talk myself out of it, I blurt, "I think I fucked up."

"Aw, girl." India reaches over to pat my arm. "What's the matter?"

"Homes's friend overheard me talking to Keto. She was saying some stuff... you know how Keto is."

"Aye." Monty leans on the counter and eyes me critically while he absentmindedly adjusts his beans. I don't think he even realizes that he's doing it anymore. "And I know that you have a habit of not speaking up when she gets out of line."

Harsh but true. I soldier on. "Well, I guess his friend told him what Keto said, and now he's mad, and we... broke up. Or whatever you do when you go from not-officially-dating to not-dating-at-all."

India waves her hand, indicating that I should continue, but I'm done. Her eyes widen, and she glances at Monty, who isn't exactly leaping to offer me the support that I was promised.

"That's it?" India asks. "There's no, like, misunderstanding element? Nothing that would, I dunno, excuse your behavior?"

"My behavior?" I repeat. "I just told you, Keto was the one who was out of line."

"Keto talks," India agrees. "A *lot.* And I'm still not sure if she says things without thinking, or if she's actively being mean, but—"

"She's a good friend," I argue, thinking of how she had my back the night of my first date with Homes. Which conveniently ignores a whole host of other things she's done on other occasions.

And which completely fails to account for the fact that when she says crappy things, I let them slide.

And still doesn't address the terrible way that Homes and I parted. The loving words I couldn't make myself say, and the hateful ones I could.

"That doesn't mean that she's right about everything." India frowns at me. "In fact, she can be kind of awful sometimes."

I frown right back. "It's not my job to educate her on how to talk to an international dish, India. She does the same thing to me."

"No, it's *not* your job to educate her. But I know how it feels when you see her saying shitty things to my face and then carrying on like it's not a big deal. How do you think Homes feels, knowing that she was saying mean things behind his back, and you just let it happen?" India lifts her chin so that she can look down her nose at me. "Because I bet you're reading from the same menu I am. You know exactly how it feels to realize that people you thought were your friends *aren't*. Don't act like you don't. If you want to spend time with someone who makes you feel bad, that's on you. But when they're talking trash about the people who matter to you, and you just sit there in silence? It makes you as bad as she is. Worse, even, because unlike Keto, I am *certain* that you know better."

I let out a grunt of frustration and turn to Monty. "I suppose you agree?"

"As a matter of fact, I do." His weary sigh drips with disappointment. "Nobody wants a partner who's a coward, Nat."

"I like Homes," I insist. "I don't agree with Keto. I would never call him a cheat food, or a guilty pleasure, or anything like that. And I don't buy into the other stuff she says, either. *I'm* not a TERB. I'm an ally."

Monty and India groan in unison.

"I'm calling BS," India says.

Monty shakes his head emphatically. "*Allies* don't let their friends run at the mouth like that, or prioritize their toxic friendships over the well-being of everyone else. Have you ever tried to correct her?"

"Well... no..." I scratch the back of my neck, remembering what I told Homes about wanting to fit in. "But I Gooed some terms."

"Whoop-de-frickin' doo." Monty spins one finger in the air and rolls his eyes. "You're really fighting the good fight, aren't you?"

I stumble back, affronted. "Excuse me?"

"You want to know something?" Monty asks. He doesn't sound angry, which is honestly worse than the alternative, because at least if he was mad, I could get mad, too. When he's disappointed, it makes me feel disappointed in myself. "My wife's ALAB."

I blink a few times.

"Assigned lunch at birth," India translates.

I press my hand to my yucca starch shell. "Really? You never said."

"Because I shouldn't have to tell you, given that it's none of your business," Monty informs me. "And to be quite honest? I wasn't sure that I should, because I wasn't sure how you'd take it. She has enough people in her life who talk about her behind her back... or who let other people say whatever they'd like, rather than rock the boat."

Everything they're saying is true, but I don't want it to be. Am I really any better than Keto? When I spoke to my parents on the phone, I kept the details of Homes's job and personal life to myself. And yeah, it wasn't any of their business, but I acted like I was ashamed of him. At the same time, he was writing a text telling me that he loved me.

He deserves better than that.

He deserves better than *me*.

"Oh my God." I sink into a crouch on the floor behind the counter, hiding my face behind my hands.

India's face appears over the top of the counter. "Is it finally sinking in?"

"I'm the worst," I mumble.

Monty snorts and rubs his fingers together. "Cry me a river, Boss. It must be *so* hard for you to realize that you've been self-serving and ignorant." This conversation has apparently unlocked his IDGAF mode, and it's a slap in the face I didn't know I needed.

"It is, but..." I cover my mouth with my hand to smother the little noise of dismay that escapes me. I was so worried about making excuses for myself that it didn't even occur to me that I was making Homes feel small the way Keto has made me feel.

I don't want to do that to anyone, least of all a person I—

Shit. Shit, shit, shit. I curl into an even smaller ball.

"I hope you didn't do this in front of Homes earlier," Monty says coolly.

"Monty?" India nudges the handle of the broom into his grasp. "Do you mind sweeping for a bit?"

With a low rumble, Monty takes the broom and stomps off into the dining room. India watches him go, then sinks down beside me to rub circles on my back.

"He hates me now." I bury my face in my apron to comfort myself with the smell of bacon and quiche.

India sighs. "Naw, Monty doesn't hate you. He's just protective of his wife. And he's definitely disappointed, which sort of makes two of us, if I'm being honest..."

I lift my head and swipe at my tears. "I wish I was like that. Protective. I wish I was the kind of person who could stand up for the people I love, even when they're not in the room. Monty's right. Letting Keto insult me makes me a coward. Letting Keto insult Homes makes me a *fucking* coward."

India chokes on a laugh. How can she find any of this amusing? I feel like my heart's been smashed like a jar of Skittles on concrete. This isn't funny at all.

"Now you're getting it," she says cheerfully. "And you get to decide who you are, right? So if you want to be the kind of person to smack some sense into your friends, then just... do that, you know? And then, bam. You're who you want to be. Like magic." She snaps her fingers and winks at me.

"Maybe." I manage to calm my breathing. Having it out with Keto wouldn't fix everything, but it would be a start. "I can try that. But I wasn't talking about Monty, anyway. I meant Homes. I bet he hates me, and I wouldn't blame him if he did."

India's smile fades as she sucks her lip. "Then I guess that's his right, don't you think? I mean, he likes you, or he *did*, but I think it would be fair if he maybe didn't trust you at the moment."

I stare down at the linoleum beneath my feet. She has a point. If Homes told me to get lost and never contact him again, I wouldn't blame him.

I find myself thinking about Keto, about the parallels between the way she's treated me and the way she's treated the other people in her life. There are good things about her, but she's far from perfect.

What would it take to make me forgive Keto for all the things she's said to me over the years? What would it take to reestablish trust between us? And if none of that was possible, would I be able to walk away from her friendship?

This fight with Homes is the catalyst, but the truth is, I should have asked myself this question ages ago. And the answer is yes. I'm willing to be honest with Keto and give our friendship one last chance. And if she isn't willing to change her behavior, then I'm not going to keep lying to myself and pretending that the way things are between us is good enough. I'd rather not have any friends than surround myself with people who bring out the worst in me.

I'm going to talk to her before I try to approach Homes again. The stakes are so much higher with him. I have so much more to lose—assuming that I haven't lost him already.

I push myself to my feet and dust off my whites. I have a restaurant to clean up.

And then I have a couple of bridges to either repair or burn.

Chapter Sixteen

I don't feel like leaving the house, but family night waits for no man, and I'd rather not explain to my parents why I don't want to come. If I told Mom what happened with Nat, she wouldn't comfort me. She'd end up taking Nat's side, and I can't handle that.

This time, I go as a ham-and-cheese wrap. I don't feel like fighting tonight.

Mom greets me at the door as a bowl of pasta carbonara, with a glass of wine one hand. "Don't you look nice!" she says.

What she really means is that I look almost how she wants me to, which is pretty depressing subtext to be perfectly honest. Compliments are supposed to make you feel good. So why do her compliments always feel like a slap across the face?

Sure enough, she pats my back a few times. "Now, was that so hard?" she asks.

"No, Mom." I drag my heels as she directs me into the kitchen, where Diner is already seated at the table. The TV blares from the den, where Dad is presumably watching a competitive cooking show.

I feel like we've done this a hundred times before, and I'm so damn tired of it.

"Hey, Homes." Diner lifts one hand in greeting. She's a bacon cheddar burger tonight, slathered in ketchup, LTO, and pickle slices. The perfect dinner daughter.

"Sit down," Mom says, urging me toward a chair. As my butt hits the seat, she raises her voice. "Meat-and-Two-Veg, your son is here! Come say hello!"

A groan of recliner springs follows, and Dad strolls into the room, all pot roast and mashed potatoes and green beans. He barely looks at me. "Hey, Homestyle. Want a beer?"

"I'm good," I say.

Dad scoffs. "A man needs a beer after a hard day at work." He pulls two cans from the fridge and carries one over to me.

"Why don't you tell your son just how *hard* your work is?" Mom demands.

Diner's eye twitches. "Actually, I have something I'd like to say—"

Dad speaks over her. "Aren't you ever going to let this go?"

"Your father is giving that slutty little Jell-O cup a promotion." Mom's smile is feral.

"For fuck's sake, Talia." Dad slams his beer down on the table. "I'm not giving her a *promotion*, okay? She was a temp. She's good at her job. I'm hiring her on. End of story."

"Dad," Diner says.

I sink down in my seat, ignoring the sweating beer that Dad handed me and that I really don't want. Screw this. I should have stayed home.

Although I guess it's better than going through my baby pictures while Mom bemoans the person I grew into.

"Maybe if you took better care of your appearance, you wouldn't be so jealous of my employees," Dad snaps.

Mom gasps. "How dare you? How *dare* you blame me for your behavior?"

"Mom." Diner keeps trying to interject. I don't know why she bothers. They've never listened. They never will.

"I haven't done anything wrong," Dad insists.

I change my mind and pop the tab on my beer, just to

remind them that I'm still here. Although if they're going to ignore Diner, their golden child, there's no chance that they'll stop arguing just because they're making *me* uncomfortable.

"Keep telling yourself that," Mom hisses. "It's one thing to lie to me, but to lie to your children..."

"They're not kids anymore, and if anyone should think about how they talk in front of them, it's you..."

Diner's voice is so loud that it echoes off the walls, drowning out their words. "Tex-Mex and I got married."

My parents freeze, their heads swiveling toward my sister in amazement. "What are you talking about?" Mom asks, the argument over Dad's secretary instantly forgotten. "You had a wedding and didn't invite us?"

"We didn't have a wedding," Diner says flatly. "We went to the courthouse, signed the paperwork, and made it official."

I whistle. "Congratulations."

Diner inhales through her nose and exhales through her mouth, doing her best to keep calm. "Thanks, Homes."

Dad stares at Diner, open mouthed, as Mom bursts into tears. "How could you do this to us?" she wails. "You're my little girl! Your father was supposed to walk you down the aisle!"

Diner glares at her. "Are you serious right now?"

"Why do my children hate me?" Mom bawls.

Diner shoots upright so fast that her chair topples. "You've got to be kidding me. I come here every week and listen to the two of you bitch and moan about the same things over and over and over again. When Homes came out as breakfast, you somehow managed to make that about you. I tell you I got married and the first words out of your mouth are about how *you* feel. I wanted to get married to the man I love without having to try to do everything *your* way. You want me to have some picture-perfect marriage, and you won't even work on your own." She stomps toward the door, leaving Mom wailing in her wake and Dad still staring at the place at the table where my sister used to be.

I'm not sure that she wants to talk to me right now, but

there's no way I'm staying there to watch my parents melt down. I hurry out the door after Diner, reaching the stoop before she's off the bottom step.

"I'm happy for you," I say.

Diner stops so abruptly that some of the ketchup splurts out of her bun. "Thanks."

"I'm sorry it went like that." I close the door behind me and trot down the steps to her.

Diner slumps against the wall of the house. "How do you stand it, Homesie?"

I study her face. "What do you mean?"

"Them." My sister glares at the front door. "It's the same every week. Every time we talk. I had this stupid idea that if I just did everything the way Mom wants, maybe she'd stop being awful to you. But it never gets better. She wants to control everything, and when she can't, she finds ways to remind other people how unhappy she is."

I shuffle my feet. "She's not that bad."

"Agree to disagree." Diner crosses her arms.

I nod back toward the house, where our mom's wailing is still audible in the distance. "Do you think Dad's sleeping with that secretary?" I ask.

"I honestly don't have a clue." Diner shrugs. "How would I know, anyhow? Dad doesn't talk to me. He's as bad as she is, in some ways."

"They're our family," I argue. Or at least, I think I'm arguing. Every time I think about dipping out of family night, this is what I tell myself.

Diner juts out her chin. "So?"

"So... we owe them?" It comes out like more of a question than I intended.

"And what do they owe us?" Diner retorts. "How unhappy are they entitled to make us, exactly? Why does being family mean that we have to let them do whatever they want, and then let them chew us out for not turning out the way they wanted? How much of ourselves would we have to change to be worthy of their love?"

I've never heard Diner talk like this. I never realized that she was just as miserable as I was. It's a good question, though, one that I never thought to ask in relation to my parents. I kept trying to fly under their radar, to be good enough that they'd forgive me for not living up to their expectations. I was doing the same thing Nat did.

Nat. It hurts to think of her. On one hand, I feel like I'm going to lose everything if I walk away from the house right now. I lost my almost-girlfriend; I can't lose my family, too.

On the other hand, the idea of going back into that house makes me sick.

"I'm hungry," I tell Diner.

She shakes her head. "I'm done. I can't take their crap any more tonight."

"Actually, I was thinking that we could go out. Just the two of us. Or invite Tex, if you think he'd like to come along. I can buy you dinner as, like, a celebration of your marriage." I hold my hands up beside my head and shake my fists, like I'm rattling maracas.

A slow smile stretches across Diner's face. "Yeah. Yeah, let's do it."

The relief that spreads through me is incalculable. I get to decide who stays in my life. I'm allowed to surround myself with people who support who I am, rather than ones who expect me to change.

For the first time since Nat and I broke up, I feel free.

Chapter Seventeen

I spend all of Monday night running through what I want to
say, and doing some research, and putting every combina-
tion of keywords that I can possibly think of into Goo. I'm
so engrossed in my quest for self-betterment that I forego my
usual bedtime.

Sometime around the witching hour, an idea occurs to me,
and I switch tracks. If I'm going to work anything out with
Homes, then I need to work on my own internalized shit just as
much as my ignorance. Homes has never complained about
working for Jo. He seems perfectly happy with what he's doing,
and with who he is. It's not like things are easy for him, either.

Oh, Christ on an unleavened cracker, I whined to *Homes*
about how hard it's been for me to fit in.

India's right. I'm worse than Keto. Every time I open my
mouth, something ignorant falls out.

It's time to start examining myself. If I can't fix things with
Homes, I'll still have to live with myself, and right now, I'm not
feeling great about the person I see in the mirror—for a lot of
reasons.

Maybe we can fix that.

. . .

Despite all my mental and emotional preparation, Keto doesn't come by after work on Tuesday for the first time in I don't know how long. Monty's still giving me the cold shoulder, but he's right. If I'm not doing the work, I shouldn't expect to be let off the hook. Once I start walking the walk, we'll work things out.

First, I need to talk to Keto. And if she won't come to me, I'll have to go to her.

It feels weird, climbing the stairs to her apartment for what may very well be the last time. I woke up this morning as *khao neow moo ping,* the same dish that my mother was when we spoke last. That feels strange, too, but also right. True, my banana leaf isn't as neatly folded as hers, and there's nori seasoning on my rice which isn't true to the Thai flavor profile, but I don't have to be just one thing. I like who I am today.

I really hope that feeling survives whatever conversation that Keto and I are about to have.

I knock on the door, my little signature rhythm. She'll know exactly who it is when she hears that beat. If she's avoiding me, then she'll know not to open the door.

Is it wrong that I'm kind of hoping she won't?

Then the handle turns, and the door swings open to reveal a chocolate-chip waffle. "Hey," Brunch says. "I'm glad you're here. She's a hot mess."

Brunch looks a lot more low key than usual. As she steps aside to let me through, I wonder about her, too. How much of a show is she putting on when she goes out in the world? Who is she at home? Is her *I have no shits left to give* demeanor real, or for the benefit of an audience?

I used to feel like I was the only one who had to shield my true self from the world around me, but now I'm starting to wonder if we're all in hiding.

Keto is on the sofa, curled up in a ball with a blanket wrapped around her. I can't tell what she is today. Only her eyes are visible through the opening in the blanket.

I stop in the doorway, marveling at the mess in her usually pristine apartment. Food wrappers are everywhere, mixed in with takeout containers, a mostly empty ice cream carton with a thin soupy sludge left in the bottom, two open bottles of wine (both chardonnay), and a cake that looks as though someone has been scooping chunks out of it with their bare hands.

"Wow," I say, because that's the only word I can force out.

"Yup," Brunch says blithely. "You missed stage one of the Breakup Protocol. Fortunately, you're just in time for stage two."

"What's stage two?" I ask.

She snorts. "Harsh truths."

"*Nooooo.*" Keto rolls sideways on the couch, curling even tighter into herself. "Please! I'm not ready!"

Brunch ignores her and keeps talking to me. "You know that EatIt thread? AITA?"

Keto's wail climbs in pitch to a wordless screech of dismay.

"She's only upset because she knows she *is* the asshole," Brunch informs me. "Pull up a chair, pour yourself a glass of whatever, and let's get down to business." She points at me. "Do you need stage two as well?"

I hold my hands up and shake my head furiously. "No, ma'am. I already got my heaping serving of uncomfortable self-reflection at work yesterday."

She sniffs. "I reserve the right to scold you more as needed. Now, Nat, you first. What did you come here to say?"

I had a whole monologue to deliver, but now that I'm here, my words have suddenly dried up. I don't like who I am with Keto. I don't like who I'm willing to become in order to win her approval. I don't like the ideas she clings to.

But she's my friend. She isn't evil. I'm certainly not perfect, either. I need to believe that I'm capable of change, that I can do better. I hope that Homes will give me the chance to prove it, and I want to extend grace to Keto, too. Whether she changes or not is up to her, and truth be told, I don't think I owe her this conversation.

I do, however, owe it to myself.

"Keto, you were the first person in this city that I could ever really call a friend." One sentence in, and I'm already off script, but I fumble through the words in the hopes of being honest with both of us. "We're pretty different, but even so, you reached out to me. You made me feel... welcome, kind of. Or at least, not outright rejected."

Brunch nods encouragingly, urging me to continue.

When I speak again, I sound more confident. "The bar was pretty low, honestly. I've been willing to twist myself up like a pretzel to get you to pay attention to me. It was like you were able to look past whatever everyone else saw and like me in spite of all that."

Brunch's brow wrinkles, and Keto nods a few times, looking a bit more hopeful than before.

I twist my fingers together, steeling myself for this next part. Now I know how Homes felt during our conversation the other night.

Honestly, it sucks.

"I don't want friends who like me in spite of myself," I tell her. "I want people to like me for who I am. Not out of charity, not out of pity, not because they think it will enhance their social status or make them feel good about themselves." My hands are shaking, and I twine my fingers back and forth, again and again, desperate to focus on something other than how terrified I am that Keto will turn her back on me, the same way I turned my back on Homes.

"Oh!" Keto's eyes well with tears. "I'm sorry, Nat, I didn't mean to—"

Before she can backpedal, Brunch holds up a hand. Evidently she's playing referee tonight. "Nope," she tells Keto, "you don't get to talk over her this time. We're using our listening ears right now."

Keto wilts back onto the couch like an old head of lettuce that got left out of the crisper.

Brunch waves her other hand to me, directing the traffic of our conversation. "Go on."

I bite my lip, grateful for the intervention, but also not sure how to proceed. Neither of the other two talks, giving me time to arrange my thoughts.

"After our conversation the other day," I murmur at last, "I went over to Homes's place."

"Was Lefty there?" Keto blurts, before Brunch side-eyes her back into silence.

"Yeah, he was. He was really hurt."

Keto whines and pulls the blanket the rest of the way over her head.

"And Homes was, too. Which was a little bit your fault, but mostly mine." My shoulders slump. Brunch watches me intently.

Keto peeks one eye out of her blanket cocoon.

"I think I ruined what we had together. It wasn't *cringe*, Keto. It wasn't *one big yike*. When I was with him, I was..." There are so many words that I could choose to describe the way Homes made me feel. Content. Sufficient. Good enough. Sexy. Desirable. Capable. Worthy. None of those words are big enough to encapsulate that ooey-gooey sensation that settled low in my belly every time he walked into a room. "When I was with Homes, I felt like *myself*. Like the mask could come off. Which was scary as hell, to be honest."

Keto's other eye appears beside its mate.

"Thinking about it now, I realize that I want to feel like that all the time." I roll my head back to stare at the ceiling so that I won't have to see how my friends respond to me. "Sometimes it'll be good, sometimes it'll be bad, but I don't want to pretend anymore. I'm never going to be happy like this. Part of me still wants to be your friend, Keto. At the same time, I don't want to be friends with someone who doesn't like *me*."

Silence fills the room, except for the hum of electronics and the rumble of traffic outside. The whole room smells like sugar, on account of all the snack foods that Keto's been eating today. I'm tempted to get up and bolt now that I've said my piece, because even though I thought this would be the scary part, it has suddenly occurred to me that whatever comes next is actually what's terrifying.

Roughly an ice age passes before Keto clears her throat. "Can I talk now?" she asks meekly.

Brunch looks to me for confirmation, and I nod.

"Um, cool." Keto lets her blankets fall away. I guess she really is having a bad day, because she's a bowl of Froot Loops, which have long since turned soggy and begun to dissolve into the milk. She's never been so vulnerable in front of me. I can't believe that this is the same person who's had so much power over me, and at the same time, I want to hug her. She shifts a few times, playing with the blanket. Probably doing the same thing I was doing with my hands, I realize. Trying to get comfortable in an uncomfortable situation.

"Well, this sucks," she says at last. "I feel like crap right now." She collapses back against the sofa, her room-temperature milk sloshing over the rim of her bowl. She's never going to get that out of the cushions. "I mean, I thought we were friends, and it turns out I've been screwing up left and right. I never meant to make you feel that way."

"Well, you did," I say.

We fall silent again. We might as well be in a vacuum sealer. All the oxygen has left the room.

Brunch claps her hands together and lets out a breath. "I know neither of you were really talking to me, although if you have something to say about how I've treated you, Nat, I hope you'll tell me." She shoots me a curious glance.

I shake my head.

"If that changes, I'm open to feedback. The question is, now what?"

I pick at my sticky rice. Keto rearranges her blanket again.

Brunch gestures to me. "Nat, what do you want from Keto? An apology?"

"I can totally apologize," Keto blurts.

I roll a few grains of my cooked rice between my fingers. "I don't know that an apology would help much. What I'd like is for her to be more respectful of me. And my employees. And Homes, whether or not we get back together. A little empathy would be great. And I'd like to know that I can point it out when you say something that hurts me or the people I care about, and have you actually make an effort to hear what I'm saying and not do it again."

Keto sinks deeper into the couch cushions with every word.

Brunch nods, like she thinks that what I'm saying is perfectly reasonable. Then she turns to Keto. "How do you feel about that?"

Damn, is this girl a life coach, or what?

"I want to be your friend, Nat." It's Keto's turn to stare at the ceiling. "And it's, like, really hard to hear all of this..."

"Imagine how I feel!" I exclaim.

Brunch arches an eyebrow at me and wags a finger. "Listening ears," she reminds me.

"I'm trying," Keto says. "I mean, God, you're one of my best friends, and I've been making you feel like this the whole time? And I was a complete beaver tail to Lefty." She groans and covers her face, pressing her palms to her eyes.

I turn to Brunch and mouth, *Beaver tail?*

"It's a Canadian thing," she whispers back.

"I guess what I'm trying to say," Keto continues, "is that I'm sorry. I don't want to be the kind of person who makes the people I like feel like crap. I didn't want you to think less of me for hooking up with Lefty, but I was the one who—*rrnnngg!*" She snatches up one of the many stark white throw pillows and screams into it. After taking a few deep breaths, she sets it aside again, and carries on as if that didn't just happen. "I was the one who thought less of myself. For what? For liking someone I couldn't imagine introducing to my parents? That's so stupid. Lefty's a great guy. He was good for me." She rolls her head forward again and finally meets my eyes. "And Homes was good for you."

"Yeah," I sigh. "But I'm not sure that we were good for either of them."

"Do you think there's any chance we could still be friends?" she asks. "You and me, I mean."

It would be great if Brunch had some answers for me, but she appears to have backed out of the conversation, giving me the space to answer that question for myself.

"I'd like to think that we aren't our worst thoughts, or our most selfish impulses." I meet Keto's eyes again. "That we aren't defined by the words uttered when we're at our most fearful and defensive. We both have a lot to learn, I think. Maybe we can help each other with that?"

Keto brightens. "Yeah. I'd like that."

"Maybe we could give our friendship kind of a test run. I'd like to talk about something I've been thinking, something I really want to do. I'm not asking for your help, I just want to talk it through..."

"I'll help." Keto scooches forward to the edge of the couch cushions, that old gleam back in her eyes. "What's the plan? Some big gesture to win Homes back? Because I can have a flash mob organized in the next, like, *hour.* I know people."

Brunch mutters something under her breath and pinches the bridge of her nose.

"No, not that." I smooth my rice over again and straighten my skewers. "I don't think a flash mob will help, and there's something I need to do before I can approach him again, anyway. Something I have to sort out for myself."

Even Brunch looks intrigued now. "Yeah? What're you thinking?"

And even though I'm terrified, I confess to the pair of them the one thing I want most in the world. After all, if I'm going to fail at something, I might as well fail spectacularly.

Chapter Eighteen

When I show up for my shift at The Daily Grind, Jo is already behind the counter pulling a double shot of espresso. We're not supposed to be open yet, but there are two people standing on the far side of the counter with their backs to me, talking to Jo in low voices. The bell over the door jingles as I step through, and the people spin toward me.

"Leftovers?" I check the clock just to make sure I'm not hallucinating. I was quiet when I left this morning so that I wouldn't wake him. He's really not a morning person.

"Hey," he grumbles. He's been in a bad mood for the last two weeks, and it's obvious why. He hasn't heard from Keto, and I haven't heard from Nat. For the first couple of days, I held my breath in the fool's hope that she would change her mind and reach out, but of course, she hasn't. Clearly, she has no regrets.

It was so damn easy for her to leave.

"What's going on?" My eyes flick from him to the woman beside him. It takes a moment for me to register that I already know her. It's Nat's other friend, the one who chewed Keto out on the day I gave Nat my number. Brunch, I think. She usually stands out in a crowd, but today she's only half a ham croissant with a drizzle of yellow mustard.

I, of course, am wheat toast. No butter. I can't think of butter without recalling Nat, and how she shivered when I greased her short stack. Everything reminds me of her, which means I'm constantly in pain.

"We're kidnapping you," Brunch says cheerfully.

"Um." I shift toward the counter. "I have work."

"Yeah, I know." Brunch nods toward Jo. "Which is why I bribed your boss to give you the morning off. I'd love to do a live stream from the coffee shop."

"Have-you-seen-how-many-followers-this-young-lady-has-Homes!" Jo pours both espresso shots into a ceramic mug, adds exactly enough milk to ensure that the mixture won't scald off her taste buds, and knocks it back in one long gulp. And here I thought she was making a drink for our customers. "So-many-followers-like-one-point-two-million-that's-a-lot-of-followers-Homes!   It-would-be-great-advertising-so-you'd-better-go-with-them-because-we-could-really-use-the-exposure!"

"Your kidnapping comes with terms," Brunch explains.

Lefty doesn't give me any indication of what's up, but if he's willing to follow Brunch wherever she's taking us, then I guess I am, too. "Is this really okay, Jo?" I ask.

My boss's smile suggests that there's more to whatever's happening here than a mere kidnapping-slash-hostage-negotiation. "Don't-make-a-habit-of-it!"

"Of being kidnapped?" I ask. I'm so confused.

"Come on," Leftovers grunts. He stalks toward the door and pushes it open without waiting for us.

"It's so nice to meet you properly, Homes." Brunch loops her arm through mine, steering me along in Lefty's wake. "I'm sorry if this is a bit out of the blue, but I had to be covert. I'm *meddling*." Her eyes glint even as a blob of her mustard smears against my crust.

"Um," I say again. "Cool?"

"You can leave if you want to, of course. But I thought you might like to see this for yourself."

She doesn't explain what *this* is, but my friend apparently knows where we're going. We travel a couple of blocks on foot until we round a corner onto one of the city's wide pedestrian boulevards.

One of the restaurants appears to be holding an event of some kind. Their tables spill out into the walkway, and people are already sitting at most of them.

"What time is it?" I check my watch. It's not even eight thirty yet, which is when The Daily Grind usually opens. What are all these people doing here so early?

That's when I see the sandwich board. *Breakfast Pop-Up. Tickets Only, No Walk-In Seating. Sorry for the Inconvenience!*

At the top of the neatly chalked board is a printed logo for Pig-in-a-Poke.

Nat's restaurant.

I stop so abruptly that I almost pull Brunch off balance. "I'm not sure I should be here," I say.

"Oh, come on." Brunch nudges me forward. "These tickets cost a fortune, and I promise you won't have to talk to her if you don't want to. She doesn't know we're here." Brunch grins as she adds in a stage-whisper, "I have an inside woman."

Lefty flops down at one of the numbered tables. I don't understand what his part in all of this is, but knowing that my presence is unexpected doesn't put me at ease. I doubt that Nat wants me here.

"I'm not sure that this is a great idea," I mumble.

Brunch hovers a hand near my back, not quite touching me. "I'm not going to make you stay, Homes. But I'd like you both to see this."

I pick at the wheat sprinkles on my crust. "This is weird. Nat and I aren't together anymore." I wince when I realize that Brunch might *never* have known we were together. If "*together*" is a word that even applies in this situation.

But Brunch nods, like this is no surprise. "I know. And if you're over her, then I won't stop you from leaving." The other possibility hangs in the air between us: that it's not over for me, that there's something I could gain by staying.

I don't move, and Brunch nods once before sidling past me and sliding into the chair across from Leftovers. I could leave right now if I wanted to.

If I do that, though, I'll never get a chance to taste Nat's cooking, and given that I've tasted the rest of her... Well, I'm curious.

Lefty grunts when I slide in beside him.

"Why are *you* here?" I ask.

He mumbles, "Moral support."

"Right." I turn away from him to scan the crowd. Plenty of the folks at the other tables are familiar, and some are even regulars at the coffee shop, but there are lots of other people I've never seen before in my life. There are a whole host of international cuisines, more than I usually see in one place. I wonder if I'm more aware of them than before, since Nat explained that she never fits in, or if the pop-up itself has something to do with the diversity of the crowd.

Two people are making the rounds at the indoor tables, and Brunch's smile lights up when they step outside. One of them is a full English, and the other is some sort of crispy folded crêpe. The crêpe spots Brunch and blurts something to her coworker, then she scurries over, skipping a few of the other tables so that she can make a beeline for ours.

"Oh my gosh, you made it!" She does a happy little shimmy of greeting, her eyes fixed on Brunch.

Lefty cracks a smile and whispers, "I think she wants to scramble Brunch's eggs, if you know what I mean."

I snort, and both of the women turn to us. Brunch waves a hand toward me. "India, this is Homes."

"I knew it!" India leans over to study my face. She clearly has no problem getting up in other people's business. She lowers her voice, checking left and right to make sure that the other customers don't hear. "To be honest, I thought you might bail. Nat feels so shitty about what went down between you two, but to be honest, that serves her right. I'm glad you're here, though."

She beams at me, then she turns to Lefty. "And you're Leftovers, right?"

Lefty smirks. "You can tell, because I'm what the cat dragged in."

India laughs, letting his bitter tone roll off her back. "Nice to meet you. We're going to be awfully busy today, so I can't hang around, sadly. I take it that you know what we're doing?"

"Er." I shake my head awkwardly. "Actually, I have no idea."

"Well, you're in for a treat!" India rubs her hands together. "Okay, so today we're offering a fixed menu." She points to a laminated tab with a QR code, standing upright from the center of the table. "You can order drinks with me, and then we'll be making three rounds with the dim sum cart. There's a whole ton of stuff to choose from, and if you miss out on anything on the first round, we'll make sure you get a chance to try it later. It's, like, small plates, right? So you can try a little of everything if you're really gung ho."

The three of us order our drinks—orange juice for Brunch, coffee for Lefty, and something called *teh tarik* for me, because why not. India writes our choices down before scurrying away, although I can't help but notice that she brushes against Brunch when she passes.

"I think I know who your inside woman is," I observe wryly.

It's not long before India returns with our drinks, and the other dish follows behind her with a two-tiered cart laden with items I only know from scanning the online menu: steaming yam cakes, tiny coconut pancakes, shallow dishes of pan-eggs with pork, cups of soy milk sprinkled with fruit, raisin-studded congee, fried omelets, mango sticky rice, shrimp dumplings, coconut cream custard...

Leftovers whistles as he studies the cart. "That all looks amazing."

Our server nods. "She's really gone all in. Never thought she'd do it, to be honest. She's been talking about it for years. What can I get you?"

"One of everything," Leftovers says without hesitation. "We'll split them."

The full English nods. "That's the right attitude."

There are chopsticks in with our silverware, and Brunch tucks in right away. Beside me, Leftovers does the same. Since when did he learn how to use chopsticks?

After a few failed attempts to pick up a piece of radish cake with my chopsticks, I give up and reach for a fork. The moment that little fried cake hits my tongue, I sigh in delight.

I don't often think about the connection between what we *eat* and who we *are*. Plenty of the time, I'm toast. It's easy, it's simple, and it doesn't bother much of anyone. As I nibble more of Nat's delectable offerings, however, it occurs to me that what I consider "standard fare" isn't necessarily the norm for everyone. How must it feel for Nat to see people pass over the dishes she loves because they're considered *exotic*? Because they want something *normal*?

Every time they're saying that about her food, they're also saying it about her.

I slam my fork back down on the table and reach for my chopsticks again. Even if Nat will never know about this, I'm going to make the effort.

"You need a hand with that?" Lefty teases as I struggle to retrieve a shrimp dumpling.

"I'm great." I take a fortifying slurp of my drink, which turns out to be a delicious milky tea. Licking the cream foam off my lips, I address Brunch. "What's the deal with this? It's new, right? I don't think Nat's ever done anything like this before."

"Well, she got a kick in the pants, didn't she?" Brunch looks over the rim of her cup and smiles at me. "I think she's fed up with playing it safe. She's being herself."

I suck in a startled breath. I don't know if that means what I think it means, but what if I was wrong? What if Nat didn't just brush off our conversation the way I assumed?

"It doesn't change how she treated you," Leftovers reminds

me, which confirms my suspicion that Brunch told him more than she's told me. "Big freakin' whoop, you know?"

Brunch catches my eye and nods toward the building. Inside, two familiar figures are standing in front of the room, dressed in chef's whites. Nat and Keto are talking to the indoor tables.

I wonder what she's saying.

Brunch is so right. I'm not over her. Not even close.

Muffled applause wafts through the windows, and Nat bows. Then she and Keto approach the doors.

I duck low. "They're coming out here!" I hiss.

"Stay the course," Leftovers replies, bracing his shoulder against mine.

Nat and Keto are talking to one another. Thinking fast, I whip my napkin up beside my face.

Lefty arches an eyebrow at me. "Subtle."

I don't care if I look like an idiot. I can't imagine having to meet Nat's gaze right now, not after the way we parted.

With her back to the windows, Nat claps her hands. She's some kind of bun today, plump and glistening, with a single freeze-dried shrimp nestled at her peak. "Hello, everyone!" she says. Her voice cracks, and she clears her throat before trying again. "Hello. I'm the chef, and I'd like to say a few words while you eat. First of all, thanks for coming out today. Your support has been incredible, and I hope we can have more events like this in the future."

A few of us applaud, and the table of shumai behind us whistles and exclaims.

Nat's smile eases. "I also wanted to say that I wish... I wish I'd done this sooner. I spent a long time thinking that people wouldn't accept me as I am. I've been told that I look weird. That I smell funky. That my textures are unpleasant. And at some point, I started to believe it. I wanted to be *normal*."

Behind her, Keto murmurs something. She looks guilty as hell.

I shift in my chair, wondering where she's going with this.

Nat shifts from foot to foot. "I'm tired of trying to hide who

I am from people who are never going to like me, no matter what I do, and losing the parts of myself that *I* like in the process. This is a dream come true, and I hope to see you here at the next pop-up event."

The applause is louder on this go-around, and it's not just the shumai getting worked up this time. A table of blintzes by the window thumps their fists on the table in approval. Brunch joins in, and even Lefty whistles and claps.

At the sound, Nat turns her head our way. I lowered my napkin while she was talking, and now her eyes meet mine. Her mouth drops open.

"*Lefty?*" Keto shoves past Nat and nearly bowls over a trio of fried plantains, who give her serious side-eye as she approaches us. She flings herself down at Lefty's feet, hands clasped between her avocado-toast chin. "Lefty, I'm so sorry. I was awful! I should never have talked about you like that, or tried to cover the fact that we were dating! The truth is, you're one of the best things that ever happened to me. Please, please, please, will you give me a chance to fix things?"

Everyone is staring at the two of them, and Lefty's eyes are huge. "Um." He drags his hand across his face, hiding his smile. "Um, I dunno, maybe. We should talk, I think. Maybe not here, though?"

Nat sidles by them and stands behind my chair, ignoring the unfolding drama. Her skin is clammy and pale, beaded with steam.

"Hey," she says softly. "You came."

I nod, because what is there to say?

Lefty helps a bawling Keto to her feet, while Brunch looks on with a small smile. I don't particularly want to see Nat sob for forgiveness, but an apology would be nice.

Instead of offering me one, however, she reaches for my hand. "Could you come with me for a minute?" she asks in a shaky voice. "You don't have to, obviously, but..."

I take her hand before she can say anything else. It's wonderful to touch her again. I don't know what any of this means, but there's no way I'm going to sit here and eat in silence, not when there's a chance that things could be different.

Her skin is warm on mine, her palm too damp while mine is too dry. It doesn't escape my notice that we're in public, where everyone can see, and she's attaching herself to me.

We leave Lefty and Keto to work their situation out as Nat tugs me inside, steering me past a smiling India to a booth beside the kitchen entrance. An older couple is sitting there, a dozen dishes in front of them. The woman looks up when we approach and immediately scrambles for her husband's hand. "*Khon dii!*" she hisses. "This is him!"

Nat and I stop short in front of the table. "Mae, Papai, I'd like you to meet—"

"*Homestyle!*" Nat's mother throws herself at me, dragging me into an awkward embrace. "Look at you! So handsome! I hope that you will make my daughter very happy."

"Thanks?" I say, incapable of both hugging a stranger and figuring out how to respond to her at the same time.

"Sit down, sit down." Nat's father flaps his hands at his wife. "You're embarrassing them." When I'm finally released from the hug, he offers me one hand to shake. "It is very nice to meet you."

Nat's smile is wary, and I realize that she's watching me more than she's watching her family. She's worried about what I'll think, or maybe how I'll react. She's worried about *my* approval, not her family's.

I didn't expect that, but I'm glad that she introduced us, even if I don't understand what it means for us. If there is an us, these days.

"It's great to meet you, too," I say. "This is pretty wonderful, isn't it? Are you in town for this event?"

Nat's mother nods. "Of course, and I am so proud. *Hee-yoo mai?*" She pats the seat next to her. "You should eat with us!"

I'm saved from answering by Keto's arrival through the door. "Nat?" she asks, twisting her fingers together. "I really don't want to flake on you, but Lefty and I need to talk. How much longer do you want me here?"

Nat bites her lip. "Um..."

"I could help," I offer.

Everyone's eyes turn toward me.

"I-i-if you want my help," I stutter. "I know my way around a kitchen, but I'll need some guidance..."

Nat reaches for my hand again. "That would be great," she says. "You can leave whenever you want, Keto."

"Thank you!" Keto hugs Nat, then me, then waves to Nat's parents before bolting out the door at top speed.

"So chivalrous," Nat's father sighs.

"So helpful," her mother adds. Both of them watch me dreamily.

"See you later." Nat smiles at her parents as she tugs my hand. "Come on, Homes. I'll show you what to do."

Chapter Nineteen

Introducing Homes to my parents has left me jittery, but there's still work to do. People want their second round of dishes, after all.

Fortunately, I've already done most of the prep, so all that's left is making sure that everything is cooked, plated, and ready to serve.

Homes is pretty good at taking directions, and while he can't keep up with me as I rush from the steamer baskets to the griddle top to the fryer, he manages to get a lot done. Whenever I reach for a clean dish, there's one at the ready. Whenever something gets emptied, he fills it before I have to ask.

Apologize, dummy. Just say the words. The trouble is, I haven't quite worked out what to say. I wasn't counting on him being here today.

We end up orbiting each other in silence, but it's easy. Companionable.

I hope I can figure my shit out before he leaves at closing time and stays gone for good.

Homes breaks the silence shortly after Monty wheels the last of the dishes through the door. "Your parents seem cool."

"They are, sometimes. And they were really happy to meet you. I, um, told them about us before... before..."

"Before we broke up?" Homes prompts. He has his back to me, intent on loading the dishwasher.

"Did we break up?" I blurt. "Or was I just a huge bitch?"

Home chokes on a surprised laugh. "Po-tay-to, po-tah-to?"

"Oh my God." I slump back against the counter. "I'm sorry. That's what I'm trying to say. I'm sorry, Homes."

He nods, but he goes back to loading the dishwasher without comment.

Say something, I think desperately, not even sure which one of us I'm talking to. I busy myself with cleaning up, kicking myself for not cooking up something more meaningful. More eloquent.

"It was nice to meet your family," Homes murmurs. "I'm surprised you told them about me."

"You're important to me. Of course I told them."

Monty bursts back in with the cart, wiping a sweaty film from his blood sausage. The baskets are mostly empty.

"Quite the promising start!" he exclaims. "I told you it was a good idea, Nat!"

"That you did."

Monty and I are still on thin ice from our fight a few weeks ago, but the moment I brought up my plans for the pop-up event, he softened. Now that Homes is standing in the kitchen with me, the last of his frosty demeanor melts. "I'm proud of you, love." He pats my shoulder. "I always knew you had it in you."

My eyes brim with tears. Even if I can't fix things with Homes, at least I have my friends. I'd rather earn their respect than keep masking who I am.

"Thanks, Monty." I wipe away a beef-scented tear.

No matter what happens, I'm glad that I gave this a shot.

It's only noon when we clear out the last of the customers and finish cleaning up. When the whole place is scrubbed and swept and sanitized, Monty and India join us in the kitchen for a milk-tea toast.

"Thanks, everyone," I say. "This is literally a dream come true. It means a lot to me that you're here."

"Well, you're paying me," India points out, but she's grinning when she says it. She keeps flicking her eyes toward Homes and making a silly little face. I know she's going to pepper me with questions later, but for now, she just finishes her drink. "Congratulations again. And I'll see you bright and early tomorrow."

"Cheers," Monty adds, tossing back his own drink.

"I'll lock up," I tell them. "We... need a minute."

Monty winks as he and India bid farewell, and then it's just me and Homes in the kitchen that's still filled with the aromas of my childhood.

I bite my lip, and Homes sets his empty glass aside, crossing the kitchen to where I stand. He takes my hand.

"Homes," I begin, just as he says, "Nat—"

Every time he touches me, my words fly out of my head. My fingers clench around his, and my heart skips a beat.

"Nat?" he repeats.

I lift my face to his and open my mouth to say—well, to say *something*, even if I'm not sure what—but before I can, his lips meet mine.

I fall into the kiss, pressing myself against his dry and crumbly exterior, bread to bread. He groans, and his hands follow the curve of my bun down to my hips. He lifts me off the floor and sets me on the counter, resting between my thighs.

I pull back and blurt, "This isn't food-safe!"

"Kitchen's closed," he rumbles.

He has a point. And to be honest, I'm not sure I can wait long enough to get home. I'm a flambé. I'm burning up.

I need him right now.

I wrap my legs around his hips, rubbing myself against his turgid crust. "I missed you so much."

"I missed you, too." He caresses my tip, where my dried-shrimp garnish is quickly rehydrating. "So much, Nat. We should talk—"

"Later," I beg.

Homes's grip on me tightens. "I'm dry, Nat. Like, super dry. I didn't bring any jam or butter or anything. I don't want to hurt you."

"I don't mind if you go in dry," I assure him. "I'm wet enough for both of us. Now, Homes. Please."

He doesn't need any more urging. His nut end sinks into me, piercing my dumpling casing. Apparently he's not familiar with soup dumplings, because he gasps in surprise when the thick, liquid pork slurry pours out of me, soaking him and dribbling down onto the floor between us.

"Fuck, Nat," he growls, "you're so juicy."

"Stop talking and focus." I lift his chin so that his eyes meet mine. I thought I was the one in control of the moment, but I'm quickly turning to jelly in his hands.

With each thrust, another gush of broth spills from between my legs. I've never squirted before. In anyone else's presence, I'd be horrified at my loss of control, but this is Homes.

My Homes.

"I love you," I gasp.

Homes sinks deep into me, spearing my beef ball through with his nobbler. As he shudders, he slips in my colloidal juices, dragging us both to the ground.

"Do you mean it?" he asks as he unwittingly sops up my secretions.

"I do," I tell him. "I love you."

He pulls me against him for a much sloppier kiss than before. "I love you, too," he says.

Chapter Twenty

❦

"Do you have everything you need?" Leftovers asks, examining the spread that he's helped me lay out.

"I think so." I study the apartment. Rose petals? Check. Candles? Check. An assortment of cheeses? Check. Champagne, lavender oil, and the small velvet box I've been hiding in my coat pocket for weeks? Check, check, check. Lefty helped me haul a ton of basil-scented candles up the stairs earlier, and we finally got them all lit.

I nibble my thumbnail as I survey the room, and Leftovers clasps my shoulder. "Hey," he says gently, "she's gonna love it."

"How do you know?" I whine. I'm terrified.

"Because she loves *you*, ding-dong." Lefty shakes me a little bit. "You can tell me that I'm right tomorrow when you share all the details. About the proposal, I mean. I don't want to hear the salacious bits, perv."

"You're the pervert." I smack Lefty away.

"Takes one to know one." Lefty's phone buzzes, and he checks the screen. "Okay, the girls are coming back from their day out. Stay strong, my dude."

"Have fun with Keto tonight," I say. The two of them have been dating off and on ever since they reconciled last year. Their fights are epic, their reconciliations legendary, their capacity for drama limitless. Lefty once confided in me that he hates arguing with her, but that the makeup sex is out of this world.

I'm just glad that my friend isn't alone. I felt bad after I moved out, but I have the sneaking suspicion that Lefty spends more time at Keto's place than he does in our old apartment. It's weird to think that we'll both move on, and someone else will take over. I wonder if they'll blame us for the fact that the carpet smells like tuna, or for the cat hair I'm always finding and can never explain.

Lefty closes the door behind him, giving me one last salacious wink before the latch clicks shut. Being alone makes me even more nervous, but before I can get too worked up, my phone buzzes with a text.

It's from my sister. *Good luck tonight, bro.*

I smile as I tap out my response. *Thanks, sis. See you and Tex for dinner Monday?*

Her response is lightning fast. *You'd better be there. And bring your fiancée !!!*

Nat's footsteps patter on the landing outside, and I tuck my phone away as she swings the door wide. She's a *biscoito de polvilho,* a Brazilian breadstick. It seems like she's a new dish every day lately.

"Hey, babe! Brunch says hi, and she was wondering if we—" Nat stops with one shoe half unlaced as she registers the candles and the spread before us. "What's all this?"

"I, um. Well, I—" I scratch my eggshell. I decided to keep it simple today, because I have big plans for later. Plans that Lefty doesn't want to hear about. "I wanted to ask you something." I drop to one knee and hold up the velvet box I've been toting around.

Nat chuckles. "Oh, gosh. This is embarrassing."

My heart drops like a stone. I could have sworn that things were going well between us. Her parents seem to love me, she and Diner get along, we've been living together for almost six months, and I thought—

Well, I thought that Lefty was right. That Nat would want this as much as I do.

Nat circles the kitchen island, digging for something in her purse until she produces a small velvet box that looks identical to the one in my palm. "I was going to ask you at the next pop-up," she admits. "The menu's Valentine-themed and everything. It was going to be pretty epic."

"I can wait!" I exclaim, scrambling back to my feet. "If you want."

Nat grins as she drops the box back into her purse. "Perfect. It's a relief to know that you'll say yes."

I slump against the counter. "Thank God. I had no idea what I was going to say. Like, I had a whole speech, but then anxiety happened. Head empty, no thoughts. Just box in the air."

"This is lovely, sweetheart." Nat plants a soft kiss on my cheek. "Thank you. We can still celebrate our, mm, our pre-engagement? Should I pop that champagne? Oh, and you got *cheeses* again." Her eyes glow bright in the candlelight, remembering the first time I came over. "I love you so much, baby."

She kisses me harder, pulling me into an embrace that feels like coming home. My head spins and my soft-boiled insides tremble.

"So." Nat pulls her head back but keeps the rest of her pressed to me. Her smile is wicked. "How do you want to celebrate?"

"Actually, I had an idea. How do you feel about dippy eggs?"

Nat's eyes widen, and she looks me over with new appreciation. "That would be a first."

"A good first?"

"I don't know, but we're about to find out." Nat shoves me toward the bedroom, and I pull her after me, laughing when I stumble against the kitchen wall. She presses me back until my shell cracks, and I gasp in pleasure, which only intensifies when she peels away a chunk of my eggshell, leaving the bare white exposed.

"Last one to the bedroom's a rotten egg," she teases, and we scramble over each other in our rush to get to the bed we share.

Even after a year, I'm startled by how much I love touching Nat—and being touched by her. When she starts peeling fragments of my shell off with her teeth, I almost hard-boil right then and there. We laugh as she rolls me back and forth, loosening the membrane that holds my remaining chunks of shell in place.

"You don't have to be so thorough," I point out.

"Of course I do." She kisses the soft spot below my jaw. "This is the first time I've ever dipped you. You better believe I'm going to do it right."

Soon enough, I'm a quivering mess, sprawled facedown on the sheets with Nat braced above me.

"Relax," she says. "And tell me if it hurts. We can stop any time, okay?"

"Mhmm." I clutch the pillow to my face and close my eyes.

When the tip of her ithyphallic breadstick starts to penetrate my white, I gasp. Nat freezes.

"Are you okay?" she asks.

"I am, I am. Keep going." I've never felt anything like it before, and the sensation only intensifies as Nat presses deeper. I cry out when her tip finally reaches my core, and I feel a little bit of my yolk slip out of me.

"Holy shit." Nat rests her forehead between my shoulder blades. "I wasn't sure that I'd be into this, but damn. Does it feel good?"

"Nat," I pant. "I... I... don't stop. Please."

Her breath is hot against the back of my neck. "I think I like it when you beg."

She picks up the pace, and with each thrust, a little more of my yolk dribbles free. I squeeze my eyes shut as the room spins. Nothing else is real, only the tumescent length of her *biscoito de polvilho* and the steam of her breath and the press of the sheets against me as she pins me to the mattress.

"Nat," I pant. "Talk to me."

"You're mine, Homes." She nips my ear. "You know that, don't you? I love you. I'm going to hit you with the most obnoxious proposal next week, in front of a whole bunch of people, and then I'm going to marry the crap out of you. I'm keeping you, Homesie. You're mine. Mine. Mine."

She doesn't stop claiming me, doesn't stop dipping me, until all of the yolk has slid out of me and only the flaccid husk of my white is left.

Afterward, she spoons me, still sticky with golden vitellus. "Are you okay?" she asks.

"Yeah." I nuzzle closer to her. "That was amazing. Is there anything I can do for you?"

"I'm good right now." She loops her arm beneath my head, holding me close. "I'm just happy to be here with you. And I could really go for some of that champagne."

"Me, too," I say, but neither of us moves just yet. Nat interlaces her fingers with mine, and we breathe deeply, enjoying each other's company. We don't need to talk. I'm just as comfortable with her in silence as I am when we talk. The last year has been amazing, and there's more where that came from. A whole lifetime of it.

I can't believe that I get to experience forever with my dreamgirl.

~

Next on the plate, so to speak, is Bigfoot Humpin':

To get some much-needed pink, he'll have to find the missing link...

Billy James Hoyt is a down-on-his-luck, red-blooded American man in 1981 rural Oregon. His mullet is perfectly kept, his farmboy muscles worked to perfection from a lifetime of construction work, and his trailer has functional plumbing. But he has no one to share it with until his eccentric best friend, Tony B Loehne, comes up with the perfect poon-hearted plan: find, seduce, and fool around with Bigfoot.

Billy is skeptical, until he gets an eyeful–and handful–of the vivacious wild woman for himself. Taken aback by the life-changing experience, but not wanting to disappoint Tony with the truth that sasquatch chose Billy instead of him, our unlikely hero has to search for the key to his wild heart while juggling an expired six-pack of lies that would churn even the most hardened roughneck's stomach.

"A triumphant masterpiece of hopeful nihilism." – My Boss

"I still love you even after reading this, and I don't know if I like what that says about me." – My Girlfriend

Hope to see you between those pages!